ANNIE JONES AND THE ANIMAL SANCTUARY

Annie Meets Molly

*"When God sends you an Angel,
you open your door and your heart."*

Written by

Tami L. Colby

ISBN: 9781737617426 (paperback)

*** Thank you to Robert St. Andrews for all of his time dedicated to editing this book.

*** I would like to Thank Heather Stiffey Simpson for taking the time to read Annie Jones while it was being written and not only offering advice but inspiring me.

*** Last but not least I would like to Thank Manon Cote and Molly. I thank you for your patience and inspiration. I also thank you for the pictures you have sent of Molly and for allowing her to be a part of my story.

Annie Jones Meets Molly

Characters:
Annie Jones- main
Sam Lee- Annie's best friend
Molly- Puggle
Simba- Annie's childhood dog
Rose Jones- Annie's mom
Ben Jones- Annie's dad
Brian Jones- Annie's brother
Jack Hennessey- Annie's Uncle
Alice Hennessey- Annie's Aunt
Joe Davis- The local Veterinarian
Florence Garcia- The Veterinarian Receptionist
Helen Brown- Annie's Mom's Friend
Sydney Brown- Helen's Husband
Gherk Brown- Helen and Ralph's Son
Emma Brown- Gherk's Daughter
Ralph Smith- Lawyer
Sally Dolan- Old college friend
Mr.& Mrs. Young- previous owners of the Animal Sanctuary
James Young- son to Mr. &Mrs. Young
Roberta Kennedy- doggy daycare owner/operator

Introduction

Annie's hometown didn't have much to offer a young girl in their late teens. It was a very small—rural town, having only one movie theater, a bowling alley, and a tiny mall consisting of only a few stores. Annie felt trapped and limited and couldn't wait to leave Murphy, Texas. Upon graduating high school, Annie left her family and Murphy behind to attend New York University and never looked back or considered returning home. She eventually graduated with honors and a degree in Journalism. She landed herself a lucrative job as a journalist at a large-reputable newspaper; where she was paid well. Annie was perfectly content to live in the big city where stores were open past nine p.m., and even open on Sundays. She loved the museums, the parks, and sometimes even the NYC nightlife.

Annie lived in Manhattan, sharing an apartment with her roommate Sam. They had lived together since both graduated from NYU: a few years ago. Annie and Sam were very close. Their friends often referred to them as a couple. They shared most of the same friends, and when they weren't working, they would go shopping together, go to movies or just stroll through the park. The only thing they didn't share as a couple was their taste in music. Annie still loved her country music. Sam would cringe whenever Annie mentioned that one of her favorite stars were in town. He told her that country music made his ears bleed. Annie was no fan of Sam's music either. She had no idea why, but he was really into the Heavy-metal, head banging stuff. Annie would mimic how someone would dance to it and laugh as Sam rolled his eyes. They were a great non-traditional couple. They spent many evenings snuggled up on their couch, watching a Netflix movie, and eating popcorn. These were Annie's favorite times. Sam was comfort — her New York family, and she loved him dearly. She wasn't sure why they weren't an actual couple as much as she loved him, and she was sure that he felt the same. It was something neither of them talked about or pursued.

Annie had met Sam in a class they had taken together in her freshman year at NYU. Corporate Communications and Public Relations was the name of the course. Annie had taken it as an elective. Sam had walked into the large classroom that day and sat down beside her. She was thankful to have him there. Sam was in his early twenties and very attractive. He had come to NYU as a transfer student from his hometown community college. He was just a few years older than Annie. He was 5'10 with a slender, athletic build. His light brown wavy hair bounced as he walked, and his eyes were a magnificent blue. Many of Annie's college friends had swooned over him while they were in college, but Annie always saw him as her best friend. *Sam's physical features hadn't changed a bit. After all of these years, he was still just as handsome as he was the first day they met.*

Annie was happy with the life she had created for herself in New York. She was living in her dream apartment that she shared with her very best friend Sam. An apartment that overlooked downtown Manhattan, where every morning she would come alive just hearing the hustle and bustle of the street. Annie never had to question if she made the right decision of giving up her life in Murphy. Although she missed her family and friends she left behind, this was the life she dreamed of having ever since she was a young girl.

CHAPTER 1

Annie Jones Gets a Phone Call

Annie was on her way to the elevator when her cell phone rang. She clutched her bags with one hand and riffled through her purse with the other. She pushed the elevator button and answered the call while she and the others waited for its' return.

"Hi mom, I am just getting on the elevator. Can I call you when I get inside the apartment?" Annie's mom responded with a whispered voice. "Annie, this is important, please call me back as soon as you can," and hung up the phone. Annie had forgotten how many times she had told her mom she would call her right back and didn't. The urgency in her mom's voice told Annie that she would need to call her mom back as soon as possible. Annie stepped off the elevator. A kind gentleman held the elevator door for her as she searched her bag for her keys. *This is ridiculous! I have got to get rid of this monstrous bag. It's not going to happen today.*

She finally stepped into the apartment that she and Sam shared: both had separate bedrooms. The apartment was not huge, but it was clean, neat, and updated. The kitchen had granite counters and all new stainless-steel appliances. Annie loved this. The ceilings were high and made the space feel much larger than it was. The living room windows were adorned with sheer curtains that ran from floor to ceiling and faced the downtown hustle and bustle that Annie loved. Although the living room was spacious enough, Annie and Sam had not splurged when they purchased their furniture. A tan sectional, a few end tables, and a desk in the corner populated the room. The most expensive piece in the room was the television. This was included at Sam's insistence. Annie didn't mind since he would be the one paying for it.

Annie sat her bags down, grabbed her phone from her purse, and made her way over to the living room window. She loved to watch the people rushing by her building. She would often find herself daydreaming about where they might be going or if they had a family at home waiting for them?

The phone rang, and she knew it was her mom calling again. "Annie, I am sorry to bother you. I was afraid you had forgotten about me. It has been twenty minutes since I called you," she replied. Annie chuckled. *Her mom had no idea what it was like to live in New York City; the elevator waits, the elevator ride, and of course, the walk to the apartment. I'm just going to leave this one alone.*

"What's up, mom," asked, "Annie. "You don't usually call in the afternoon, and your phone call sounded urgent?"

"Annie, your Uncle Jack has passed away, and his wife, your Aunt Alice, would like to have everything finalized this weekend; the viewing at the funeral parlor, the graveside service, and the reading of the will. She requested that you be here for all three." replied Annie's mom.

Annie set the phone down. She hadn't thought about her Uncle Jack since moving to New York seven years ago. He always sent her a Christmas and Birthday card every year – since she had left. He would usually attach a heartfelt note, telling her how much he missed her. He thought that one day he could convince her to move back.

Annie hadn't been home to visit since her mother's sixtieth birthday party: four years ago. The phone call from her mom, telling of her Uncle Jack's death, forced her to face the return to her small hometown. She had come to associate with boredom.

Jack was Annie's Uncle from her mother's side of the family. He was the older brother and often tried to help care for his younger sister Rose – Annie's mom. Their relationship was the typical elder brother and younger sister scenario. Jack would always try to look after his little sister. Rose would have to remind him that she was a grown woman and could look after herself. Besides, she had been married to Ben, Annie's dad, most of her adult life.

Annie's Uncle Jack had been out of town for an emergency at the time of her mother's birthday party. He and his wife — Alice, were in California visiting Alice's mother who had fallen ill… Uncle Jack had always been a little husky, but his six-foot four-inch frame enabled him to hide his few extra pounds. He and Rose shared the same black-wavy hair: his hair being shorter. Jack was a true Texan through and through. He never left the house without his cowboy hat, cowboy boots, and, most notably, his Colt Python pistol that he carried in a hip holster. Jack was old- fashioned, courteous, and always looked after the ladies. This behavior would often cause rifts between him and Alice.

Annie never cared much for her Aunt Alice, but she never let anyone know, especially her Uncle Jack. She spent a lot of time on their farm as a young girl, and Alice was part of that package. Alice was a rich girl from the city; she came from old money. Her maternal grandparents were real estate investors and accumulated their wealth by buying large tracts of under-valued land throughout Texas, holding the deeds until their market value increased. Her grandfather would then sell the land to developers and oil prospectors. The profits were huge, and eventually, the family became one of the wealthiest in Northern Texas.

Alice's mother lived a life of luxury and privilege, as did Alice. Alice's grandparents had passed when she was a young child, but she could still remember the visits with her papa and could still remember the smell of his pipe that he would smoke on occasion.

Alice recalls him telling her on numerous occasions that one day this could all be hers, although, at that time, Alice had no idea what he meant.

Alice's parents had looked forward to their only child marrying one day. They expected her to find a husband that came from a family of equal financial stature. The merging of two such families would ensure their wealth and prestige for many generations to come. Her parents were less than thrilled when they learned of Alice's desire to marry Jack, especially at such an early age. Jack was only eighteen years old when he proposed to Alice. They both had just graduated from high school. Jack's father was a dairy farmer, and Jack planned to follow in his father's footsteps. The farm had been in the family for generations. It didn't make them a lot of money, but it paid the bills and allowed for a little extra at the end of the day. Jack's father was getting older, and Jack enjoyed spending the time with him and learning from him.

Alice's parents tried to explain to her what she would be giving up by marrying Jack. They even went so far as to convince her that Jack was after their family's money and power. However, Alice was in love with Jack, and that was all that mattered to her. They warned her that if she chose to marry him, against their wishes, she would not receive any financial help from them. They would cut her off. Luckily for Alice – her grandfather's written will guaranteed Alice's inheritance of all family assets upon her parent's death.

Alice was in love with Jack. She just assumed that he would be able to support her and the lifestyle she had been accustomed. Annie witnessed several arguments throughout the years between the two of them over money or should I say, their lack of money.

Annie loved her Uncle Jack. As a young girl, they were very close. She smiled, remembering how he would dance his way through the door, and grab her by the waist. He'd lift her and dance around the kitchen as she squealed with delight while her mother, Rose looked on and chuckled. He would often bring Annie to his horse farm. She would saddle-up Patches her favorite horse, and ride for hours. "You're a natural cowgirl," he would tell her. When the riding was over, Annie would help her Uncle clean out the stalls, feed the chickens, and care for the many puppies Jack always seemed to have around. Annie was always amazed and delighted by the number of pups Uncle Jack kept. This was a special time in her life.

Annie remembered the many times that her Uncle would tell her, "Animals are Angels sent to us from heaven. They offer unconditional love, and we should offer them a warm – loving home whenever possible." Uncle Jack believed that. He always had several dogs, cats, chickens, horses, despite his wife's many objections.

Annie had always loved animals. As a young girl, she longed for a pup of her very own. However, her mother was allergic to most animal hair. Having an animal was out of the question. Annie often wondered if her mother's allergies were exaggerated. She wasn't much of an animal person.

Annie loved those days on her Uncle Jack's farm. She would often spend large chunks of her summer vacations there. She loved being close to her Uncle Jack, and his animals. Jack lived on the farm with Alice, his wife, and high school sweetheart. Although Annie didn't care much for her, she was always polite for Uncle Jack's sake. She felt terrible for her Uncle Jack. He always wanted children, but Alice never did. Perhaps, that is why he surrounded himself with so many animals. Maybe in some way, they helped to fill the void. Alice did not want children, nor did she have any use for Jack's animals. Annie could remember countless arguments between the two of them: over the animals. Much to Annie's surprise, Uncle Jack almost always won the debate.

Annie had been especially fond of her Uncle Jack's pups. He had many of them over the years, and their many different personalities amused her. The eldest dog, at the time, was named Duke. He must have been at least ten years old – the last time she saw him. Duke was a stray that had wandered onto her Uncle Jack's porch one day. His short dark brown short hair had been all matted. It was clear he had been severely malnourished. Uncle Jack wasn't sure how Duke found his way to the farm, and it didn't really matter much; he would never turn away an animal in need and would often say:

"When God sends you an Angel, you open your door and your heart," he always said.

After Duke spent a few months on the farm, it became apparent that he was the alpha male. He was a Pit-bull-Rottweiler mix and perhaps even a little retriever, since fetch was his favorite thing to do. He'd retrieve anything and everything Uncle Jack asked him to. Jack used to say that the retrieving thing was Duke's way of expressing his gratitude for my saving him. Annie believed that to be true. Duke was loyal to Uncle Jack, and you could find them joined at the hip most of the time. Duke would ride along in the truck when Jack came to pick Annie up. He would sit straight up between her and Uncle Jack: giving her wet – slobbering kisses when she got in the truck. Annie, never having a dog herself, would giggle at the way Duke looked so human-like, sitting in that truck. She stopped and thought for a moment; She wondered, *was Duke still alive? It didn't seem likely; Uncle Jack would have told her if he passed... or would he?*

The second dog in line, going by age, at that time, that she could still recall was Jasper. Jasper was a chocolate lab, and probably around eight or nine years old at that time. Uncle Jack had Jasper since he was a pup, and Annie loved him. He would run up and greet her with a dirty, slobber covered tennis ball and insist she throw for him. She remembered how he would usually get sidetracked and not make it back with the ball until hours later: she would just laugh.

Then there was Rosa and Mia. Annie wasn't sure of their ages but she knew they came from the same litter and just happened to appear one day at the farm. One day shortly after their arrival, Annie happened to be petting Rosa and found a scar along Rosa's neck. It was a deep scar. Annie was sure that at one time, it had been a bad one. She looked at her Uncle Jack, and he knew the question before she had to ask. Annie, being a young girl, prompted Jack to proceed cautiously. "Well, Annie," said Jack, "It's a long story, and I promise to tell you one day. Let's just enjoy those happy faces and wiggly tails for now." Annie shrugged her shoulders in agreement. She never did get to hear that story.

Simba was the last, but surely not the least, of the pups. Annie remembered his name because of the Lion King movie that had just come out. During one of her week-long visits, Uncle Jack had taken her to see the film. Long story short– later that week, her Uncle Jack showed up, at the farm, with a puppy. A teeny tiny puppy. Annie remembered how she shrieked with excitement. She recalled how Jack had so gently placed this little Pup into Annie's arms and how she felt so much love – so quickly.

There was no doubt in her mind: Simba would be his name. Annie whispered her choice to Uncle Jack – looking for his approval.

"Whatever you wish, Annie," said Jack. "Simba is yours to take care of whenever you are here. I expect that you will take excellent care of him and give him all of the love he deserves."

Annie wiped the tears from her cheek. Just thinking of that day made cry. *It was funny that her Uncle Jack never mentioned Simba in any of the notes he would send to her every year for*

Christmas and her Birthday. She felt a twinge in her belly: it was guilt. She let Simba and her Uncle Jack down.

Given that Annie was twelve years old when Simba was a pup, she estimated his current age to be around twelve years old. She wondered if he might still be alive. Annie decided to visit the farm and If, in fact, he was still alive, she needed to explain to him why she left and apologize for abandoning him. She was overcome with guilt and began to cry uncontrollably at the thought of what she had done. She realized that Simba had lost his closest friend, companion and had no idea why she left.

Annie was glad Sam was at work today, and she had the apartment to herself. She usually wasn't so emotional — like this, and Annie wasn't sure when it was going to stop. She thought for a moment. She recalled several other pups that had lived on Uncle Jack's farm. She just couldn't remember all of their names. There was a time when she had all their names memorized and she treated each one like the unique angel they were. Annie decided she could not take the pain reminiscing brought her anymore. She grabbed her jacket and made her way to the city streets of Manhattan. Perhaps, a little downtown shopping would ease the pain.

Annie stopped by a little boutique, a block from her apartment. If she were going home – she might as well bring a few gifts along. She remembered that her mom loved fairies. After careful consideration, she decided on a necklace. It was a fairy sitting on a half-moon, and the stone in the center was her mom's birthstone: amethyst.

The shopping had a therapeutic effect on Annie. She was finally able to shake off her feelings of guilt and sadness. As she walked around the city, she found a candy shop. She filled a bag with her father's favorite nut clusters. He was never the easiest man to buy a gift for. Annie looked at her watch and realized Sam would be home soon. She turned around and headed back toward the apartment. She would have to tell Sam about her Uncle's death and that she would be out of town for a few days.

Annie thought it would be a good idea for them to have dinner out at the last minute. She made a quick call to Sam. They agreed to meet at the Bistro on the corner. Sam was Annie's best friend, and she knew many people wondered why they weren't more than friends. Annie never had the right answer. She would simply answer, "he is my best friend: that's why."

Annie told Sam about the day's events. She told him she would be leaving town for a few days. Sam offered to go with her, but Annie declined. "Sam, this is going to be a quick trip. I'll be back by Monday. There is no reason for you to come along," she explained. Sam nodded in agreement. He was a little disappointed that his best friend didn't need him, but he understood.

CHAPTER 2

Annie Flies Back to Her Hometown

The next morning Annie caught a cab to the airport. Traffic was light this time of the day and, Annie arrived at the airport well ahead of her departure time. She had plenty of time to check her baggage in and relax before boarding the plane. Her flight was uneventful, and when she arrived at the Dallas-Fort Worth airport, her mom and dad were waiting to greet her.

Annie dreaded going back to her small hometown. Many of Murphy's homes were surrounded by farm fields, and two-lane winding roads leading to more farm fields. The only stores in town were Albertson's grocery, the Dollar Tree, and an antique store that never seemed to be open. Cobblestone streets and sidewalks gave the sleepy little town a warm and comfy feel but It was not New York City. Annie was hoping the downtown shopping options had expanded since the last time she visited.

Annie's mom spotted her and ran up to her, giving her a big hug as soon as she arrived, followed by a hug from her dad. Annie was daddy's little girl, and he was happily wrapped around her finger. Annie's brother Brian, who was waiting for them at the house, was ten years younger than her. He was now in junior in high school and, from what she had heard, entirely independent.

Annie's dad grabbed her bags, and the three of them moved through the crowd as quickly as possible. It was a half-mile walk back to the parking garage where her dad had parked. Annie's dad loaded her bags into the trunk. Annie felt small, climbing into the backseat of her dad's car. She hadn't done that in quite some time. Annie's mom made small talk about the new neighbors down the road. She went on to tell Annie about their kids, grandkids, and what they did for a living. Annie couldn't help but let her mind wander.

Dallas hasn't changed much, Annie thought to herself as her mind drifted away from her mother's chatter. She didn't mind the crowd of people or the enormous amount of traffic. She had become accustomed to the hustle and bustle – city life, having lived in New York City for so many years. But Annie's parents were the opposite. They had no use for this environment. Annie could already sense the tension in her mom's voice. She was thankful it was her father driving back to the house and not her mother.

There was one main road, a four-lane highway that led from Dallas to the town of Murphy. Annie looked behind her as her father sped up to keep up with the flow of the traffic. She smiled when she heard her mother yelping in her dad's ear to slow down. Her mother never drove much, and she would never attempt to drive into Dallas. Annie admired the skyscrapers and the beautiful landscaping surrounding them as they whizzed by. She was amazed at how well kept the sides of the highway were. There was no garbage, and the lawns were perfectly manicured.

The town of Murphy was about twenty-five miles away from Dallas. Ben caught the exit that led to Murphy; the road was winding and surrounded by farmland on both sides. For the first time, Annie admired the peacefulness of the country road. *Maybe she needed some time to slow down.* She caught a glimpse of some children playing in the field. She was surprised at herself – that she would even notice something so trivial. It was as though she was looking at the town through a new lens.

They drove past the old Murphy Estate. Annie couldn't recall how many years it had been vacant. The fields had grown over so much that it was difficult to see the house, from the road. They drove past the small cemetery. There were approximately thirty graves planted near the house. It was surrounded by trees and a gated fence that had been kept under lock and key for years. Annie was surprised at how well-kept the cemetery was as they rode past it. The house seemed to be untouched. The paint was flaking and the shutters barely hung from the windows, it was evident that no one had cared for the old place in a very long time.

Annie remembered her papa telling her about the Murphy family. They were one of the early settlers: arriving around 1846. At one time, the town had been called Maxwell's Branch. After the Saint Louis- South Western Railway reached the area, the residents changed the name to Murphy, suggesting it was named after William Murphy, who provided land for the depot's tracks and construction. It has been known as Murphy ever since.

Annie's mind began to wander, *wow Brian was a Junior, he'll graduate next year.* She wondered what his plans were after he graduated. Selfishly, she was hoping that he planned on staying close and not move away, as she did years before. Annie felt a tinge of guilt again. *"Why don't I talk to mom as often as I should? How could it be that I don't even know my own brother's plans after high school?* Annie felt ashamed. *She always intended to call her mom more; she was just always busy with her own life.*

Annie was hoping this car ride wouldn't last much longer. All of her thinking was just leading to more guilty feelings. She wondered: *Have I always been this selfish and self-centered?* Annie was about to ponder that idea a little further when her dad pulled into the driveway. She was surprised at how seeing her childhood- home made her smile. Annie got out of the car and was amazed at how little had changed. The old house with its wrap-around porch was beautiful. Her dad had always taken impeccable care of the old ranch-style house. There was a beautifully landscaped walkway that her mom had put in years ago: before Annie had left for school. Now, there were beautiful daffodils along each side.

Annie was on her way inside when her brother Brian stepped out of the house, he ran over and picked her up – swinging her around as if she were a rag doll. Annie was the runt of the family. She was 5'2 and usually ran around 105 lbs. on an average day. She felt lucky that, over the years, her physique hadn't changed much. She worked out at the gym occasionally with Sam, but she knew that genetics allowed her to maintain herself so easily. Her blonde hair and hazel eyes came from her dad's side of the family. When she was growing up, folks would joke that there was no doubt she was Ben Jone's daughter. If Annie had been born a boy, she could have passed as Ben's twin. Her brother Brian most resembled their mom. He had jet black hair, and his eyes were the bluest Annie had ever seen. She often wondered where those deep blue eyes came from since their momma's eyes were more of a light blue.

Annie was shocked to see how much Brian had grown. *Had it been that long?* Brian was only Thirteen years old when she last saw him. It was her mother's sixtieth birthday party. There it was again, that tinge, in her belly, reminding her of just how selfish she was. Annie was always so busy with work. Every time she and Sam had planned to visit, something would come up, and they would have to reschedule. It was never her intention to stay away as long as she had; it just seemed to work out that way. Brian had grown into a man, and she had missed it. He had grown to be at least six-foot. Brian reminded Annie of her Uncle Jack. Like Jack, he loved his cowboy hats and boots. Annie knew that one day he would be carrying a pistol, as well. He was also incredibly handsome, just like their Uncle Jack. She imagined the girls at school were falling all over him. Annie smiled at the thought of it. Brian finally set her back on the ground and ushered her into the house. "Annie, I'll grab your bags from the car and bring them to your room, and then we can catch up," he yelled through the door.

Annie walked slowly up the stairs to her room at the end of the hall and opened the perfectly manicured wooden door. It looked to be recently refinished. She could feel the goose-bumps rise on her arms as she walked in her childhood room. It was surreal, like taking a step back in time. The only thing that had changed was her. It was funny how her mom had kept her bedroom the same after all these years. Annie's head was swirling with memories. She ran her fingers along the wall.

She and her mom had painted her room when she was in the ninth grade. Annie had been going through a phase and had decided pink was her least favorite color. And of course, until that day, everything had to be pink – including her bedroom.

Annie remembered the weekend she and her mom spent repainting the room. After many color rejections, from her mom, they agreed on a pale yellow. Annie was pleased with that decision then, and as she walked around the room; she still felt the same way. Yellow was the perfect color for this room. Annie's eyes glanced over all the trophies she had collected through the years. She was never one to brag about her awards, but she loved to display them in her room. She stretched out onto the queen-sized bed. Annie remembered how she had talked to her mom and dad into buying it. The pale-yellow comforter was splattered with tiny white flowers, and it matched the walls nicely. The bed had a warm, inviting feeling, and Annie was looking forward to burying herself into her bed later that night. She left for school a few years later so the bed barely used, was like brand new.

A few moments later, Annie heard footsteps coming up the stairs. She was sure it was her brother Brian, the footsteps were moving quite quickly, and she was sure he had even skipped a few steps here and there. There was a knock at the door, and she heard her brother's voice. "Annie, your bags are in the hallway. I have to run an errand, but I'll be back later, and we'll catch up then," Brian yelled as he ran back down the stairs.

Annie was almost relieved that Brian had somewhere else to be; seeing him, all grown up, just reminded her of how guilty she felt – deep down. She didn't understand why she never had any of these feelings before her Uncle Jack's death.

Annie's mom invited a few of her close friends over and asked Annie to join them. Annie was happy to oblige, and sitting outside, on their wrap-around porch, reminiscing was kind of fun. After several hours of chit chat and a gourmet meal prepared by her mom, Annie said goodnight and made her way upstairs. She looked forward to stretching out on the queen-sized bed that had been calling her all day. Annie had forgotten how quiet the night could be: living in the country. There was no traffic, no neighbors, no noise, and she drifted off within a few minutes. The day had been fun but exhausting.

The next few days were going to be busy for Annie and her family. Jack's wife, Alice, wanted everything finalized that weekend. First, would be the funeral service, followed by a small ceremony at the cemetery. Annie had no idea just how many hearts and lives her Uncle Jack had touched. She found herself surrounded by many people she didn't know and many names she had never heard. She listened to so many stories about her Uncle Jack; it was as if he was there with them.

CHAPTER 3

—◆—

The Reading of the Will

Friday and Saturday went by like the blink of an eye. Sunday was the final ceremony: the reading of Uncle Jack's will. It appeared that Uncle Jack had more money than he had let anyone know, and everyone lined up for their piece of the pie. Unlike the rest of them, Annie was only there to hear the reading of the will at her Aunt Alice's and her mom's insistence. She sat and waited as everyone else proceeded. She was surprised that she was even in her Uncle Jack's Will. She hadn't seen him in at least seven years.

At Annie's request, the lawyer read her Uncle's wishes to her in private. There was no need for everyone else to be privy to such a personal thing. Ralph, Uncle Jack's Lawyer, began to read Jack's wishes. The note her Uncle had left her explained that Jack had been sick for months. He knew he was going to die and prepared as much as he could in advance.

Uncle Jack wrote, "My dear Annie, it has been so many years since you left your childhood-home town. I can't help

18

but remember our happy times – when you would visit the horse farm. You would ride for hours, help clean the stables, and feed the chickens, but most of all, I remember how you loved every one of our dogs. You would make sure to kiss and hug each of them when you arrived and left. Annie, you have such a big heart, but I think you have forgotten the essential things in life. I hope you remember what I told you about animals; they are Angels from Heaven and are the only creatures in this world that will give you unconditional love. I know it was hard for you to grow up without a pet. That is why I have decided to leave you the Animal Sanctuary. It was a purchase I made for you before you left for New York, and up until now, I didn't know quite how to tell you. Before you have a chance to speak your mind: as I know you will. You need to know one more thing. There is no one in this world; I would trust more with my beloved dog Molly, than you. Please take her and give her the best of everything, she deserves it, and the rewards that will come your way will be two-fold, all of my love, Uncle Jack."

Annie sat silent for a few moments. For the first time in her life, she was speechless. *I cannot believe this is happening to me.* Of course, this Animal Sanctuary was not far from her mom's and dad's house in her childhood town. Annie was no longer speechless. She began to yell at the lawyer, sitting behind the desk, as though he had just ruined her life. Annie began to pace the floor, "He cannot do this to me, can he?" she asked the lawyer.

"These are your Uncle Jack's wishes," responded the lawyer." If you don't want the place – you could sell it or hire someone else to run it? As far as Jack's dog is concerned, I recommend bringing her with you wherever you go. Molly was your Uncle Jack's pride and joy. He would not have left her with you if he didn't think you would take the very best care of her."

"Annie, you have until Tuesday to make your decision; I hope you'll make the right one." Annie was furious at the lawyer's last comment. She stood up, walked to the door, and slammed it behind her. She was headed down the hallway when the lawyer opened his door and yelled, "Annie, I understand your feelings about the Sanctuary, but please don't forget about Molly. She has been in the backroom waiting, all of this time, for you to bring her home."

"Why me?" She stormed back into his office, muttering.

"I'll be right back," said Ralph as he escaped behind closed doors.

It was only minutes later and Uncle Jack's lawyer strolled out, with the now infamous Molly. Annie had to hold back her laughter. This pup could not possibly be one of Uncle Jack's. Even if Jack had a female dog, Annie was quite sure she wouldn't look like this one.

"You have to be kidding me," Annie said to the lawyer with a smirk.

"I can assure you," said the lawyer with a smile on his face. "I have known your Uncle for years, and for at least the past six months, he has had Molly with him every time he came into the office."

The lawyer led Molly over to the same chair that Annie had sat. Molly was a small dog. Like the rest of her body, her face wrinkly, and her large brown eyes were as round as could be. Annie couldn't be sure what kind of pup this was, but before she could even ask, the lawyer responded, "I suppose you are wondering what type of breed Molly is? Well, Annie, Molly is a

Puggle. She is part Pug and part Beagle," Annie was reluctant to ask the next question, but since the lawyer seemed to know a lot more about her Uncle Jack than she did: she couldn't resist.

"Well, asked Annie. "Is there any reason Molly is wearing a pink sweater, matching booties, and headband – with a bow on her head? Did Uncle Jack dress her this way, or is this some kind of joke?"

The lawyer couldn't help but chuckle before he replied, "Annie, this is not a joke. Your Uncle Jack has dressed Molly this way for as long as they have been coming to this office. He loved Molly more than anything on earth, probably more than your Aunt Alice. Please don't tell her I said that."

Molly walked up to Annie's hand and pushed it as if to ask to be petted. It had been many years since Annie had come in such close contact with any animal. She had forgotten how soft their fur felt as she moved it through her fingers. Molly looked sad. *Did she miss Uncle Jack?* Annie wondered.

"Okay, now that you two have warmed up to each other, there are two more things we need to take care of before you leave," said Ralph.

"Seriously?" asked Annie. Haven't we shared enough for one day?" The lawyer just smiled and reminded Annie, "Your Uncle made all of these arrangements' months ago. He had plenty of chances to change his mind: he never did."

Annie sat and waited for the lawyer. "He's trying to ruin my life. I know it," she said out loud.

"I'll be right back," the lawyer said, as he disappeared once again. He was gone for only a moment. When he returned, he had two large suitcases. Annie gasped at the size of the bags. She was not a world traveler herself, but she had never seen suitcases so large.

"These bags are full of Molly's wardrobe. I didn't bring them out earlier because I wanted to be sure you were taking her," explained Ralph.

Annie's eyes lit up if only for a moment. "If I'm taking her? Do you mean there is someone else in line to take her if I should choose not to?" Annie was a little excited. Although she loved animals, she had never taken care of one on her own, let alone a Diva like Molly.

The lawyer replied with a hesitation in his voice. "Yes, Annie; Your Uncle Jack knew there was a chance you would say no, he had to prepare for the worst.

Annie had to ask the question, although she was already becoming fond of the little Diva. "Let us suppose I don't take Molly," said Annie. "Who would she live with?" Annie held her breath; she was afraid of what he might say.

"Your Uncle Jack has made arrangements with the folks down the road. They were his last resort; they are not in the best of health. Henry is eighty-three years old, and his wife Wilma is eighty. They were very close to your Uncle Jack, and Molly as well. He would never have suggested it, but they insisted rather than see Molly go to the shelter."

Annie lowered her head as if defeated. "Well, I would like to say it was nice doing business with you today but, that would be a lie. I feel as though my life has entered a whirlwind, and I just don't think I can take any more news today." She looked down at Molly and said, "Let's go, girl; if Uncle Jack wanted you to be with me, he must have had his reasons."

How did Uncle Jack forget that momma was allergic to animal hair: all animal hair? It was indeed going to be interesting?

"Annie, before you leave, as I mentioned, there is still one more thing," the lawyer whispered – as softly as he could. He knew he was on Annie's last nerve. Lawyers, like him, always save the best for last. Annie rolled her eyes. She had heard enough of "one more thing" for today. She was ready to go, but before she could get out of her chair, the lawyer handed her the envelope and said, "Annie, this is for you from your Uncle Jack."

At this point, she was afraid to open anything from her Uncle. The entire day it was filled with nothing but crazy – unexpected events. The lawyer sat there as if his day's ending was not complete until she opened the letter. Annie slid her fingers across the top of the envelope, being careful not to tear anything inside. She reached inside and pulled out the paper. It was some form of a legal document listing Annie as the beneficiary. The first part of the paperwork was the deed to the Animal Sanctuary; the second part was much more of a surprise. She read the second half out loud, just be sure she was reading it correctly.

On behalf of myself, Jack Hennessey, I do, as of this moment, leave three hundred thousand dollars to the custodial caregiver of my pup: Molly. This money is to be used to be sure that Molly has the best life possible. Upon Molly's death, any funds left over shall remain with the custodial caregiver to use any way they choose: signed Jack Hennessey.

Annie was speechless. Her Uncle Jack had done it again. By this time, her head was reeling, and she was ready for some much-needed rest. She still had the pleasure of going home and telling her mom that Molly would be staying with them until she could catch a flight back to New York.

Annie proceeded to leave the lawyer's office, this time – a friendly handshake, and she and Molly would be on their way. Ralph yelled as they walked to the parking lot, "I look forward to hearing from you on Tuesday."

Annie lifted Molly to put her in the front passenger seat. She pulled out her cell phone and dialed Sam's number, as she saw that he had called five times today. *He is probably wondering what happened to me; this meeting was supposed only to take a few hours but ended up being most of the afternoon.* She dialed his number, and he picked up on the first ring. "I've been calling you for hours!" Sam shouted, "I was worried that something happened to you!" Annie chuckled to herself. *Something had happened to her, alright.* "Too much to talk about right now, Sam. One thing I can tell you is that we have inherited a pup, not just any pup; this little girl is a Diva. Sam, I have to go. I promise I will call you just as soon as I can, but I will be staying here at least another few days."

Annie hung up the phone. She was happy to have left the conversation where she did. She hadn't even decided if this Animal Sanctuary thing was something she wanted. She would go there tomorrow to see if; this is worth keeping.

Annie and Molly went back to her parent's house. Annie's mom began sneezing when they walked through the door. "I am so sorry, mom, Molly, was Uncle Jack's pride and joy, and he thought I was the best fit for her for some unknown reason."

"We can keep her in the study for now until you take her upstairs for the night," said Annie's mom.

Annie planned to visit this so-called Animal Sanctuary in the morning and then make her decision. She had so much to consider, *would she want to leave her home in New York, and what about Sam? He was her best friend. Was she willing to go without him?* These were some significant factors to consider. Annie had so much to think about before making any decisions.

Annie just wanted to grab a bite to eat and hit the hay. She sat at the kitchen table, going over the day's events with her mom, but she was so exhausted from the day, she just wanted to stop talking and head for the bedroom. Annie went to the study to grab Molly. She walked in and saw her curled in one of her dad's favorite chairs. Annie wondered if Molly could sense what was going on and if Molly missed her Uncle Jack? Poor Molly, she thought to herself. "Come on, little girl," said Annie, as she rustled her out the chair. "Time for you to go potty outside, and then it's off to bed we go."

Molly looked up at her with sleepy eyes. Annie knew she must have been exhausted, confused, and probably sad.

CHAPTER 4

Annie And Molly Get Acquainted

The next morning Annie jumped out of bed, her mind still reeling from yesterday's events. She had been so tired last night that she passed out as soon as her head hit the pillow. Annie sat up and looked around. At first, she didn't see Molly and felt a tinge of concern in her belly. She wondered if that would now be a frequent feeling. She was now a mother. Annie chuckled as she looked down at the floor, and she saw Molly sleeping in her little pink bed: with Diva sewn across the front. *Uncle Jack had lost his mind when it came to his precious Molly. It was clear that she meant everything to him.*

"Thanks, Uncle Jack!" Annie yelled up at the ceiling above her as if expecting some response.

Annie grabbed Molly and ran down the stairs; her dad had made a temporary lead for Molly off the back porch. She was getting used to the new home and family. Annie watched as she sniffed around the area for the perfect place to do her business. She must have been too tired to explore last night. She was making up for it this morning.

"You do your business, little girl, bark when you are ready to come back in," Annie instructed her.

Annie grabbed a bowl of cereal and sat down at the table. Her mom and dad were already up. They were excited to see Uncle Jack's gift to Annie. They were hoping that she might finally move back to her hometown and visit with them regularly. In the meantime, while Molly was doing her business outside. Annie grabbed the list of instructions from her Uncle Jack, detailing Molly's food, her treats, her schedule, and, finally, her outfits. Yes, this little girl was a Diva. She heard a bark and went to get Molly from the lead. She whipped up Molly's special breakfast, one scrambled egg, and one turkey sausage. "Come on, girl, let's get you some breakfast and start our day," said Annie. Molly devoured her dish within seconds. Annie didn't think she had ever seen a pup eat so fast. Molly had a curvy figure, and judging from her physique, she obviously ate well.

Annie decided it would be the perfect morning for Molly to have a bath. She had never bathed a dog before, but she assumed the instructions left from her Uncle would include a section on bathing and grooming. Annie grabbed the instruction book from the counter and rifled through the pages. She was so excited when she finally got to the grooming page and read the section on bathing. Uncle Jack wrote out a full list of do's and don'ts, not only for baths but for grooming in general. "Come on, Molly!" Annie yelled as she ran up the stairs. Molly trotted behind her. It was clear they were going to be inseparable, just the way Uncle Jack had wanted it.

Annie sifted through Molly's belongings in hopes that there would be at least one bottle of dog shampoo. She had already decided if she could not find one, they would be taking a trip to the pet store. Luckily, after a few moments – of searching every side pocket, she pulled out a small bottle, "Look, Molly, dog shampoo!" Molly wagged her tail excitedly. *Did she recognized the bottle, or was she just excited because of the sound I made?*

Annie grabbed the book of instructions from the bed, and they made their way to the bathroom. Molly sat patiently on the floor as she watched Annie filled the tub with water. "I hope this goes well," Annie whispered. She lifted Molly and placed her into the tub. Molly splashed around like a fish out of water. "Molly girl, you are not making this easy for me!" Annie cried as Molly continued jumping and splashing around in the water.

Annie wasn't sure how it happened, but within seconds Molly, covered from head to toe in doggy shampoo, jumped out of the tub and ran down the stairs. Annie, soaking wet herself, ran as quickly as she could to catch up to her. Annie saw her mother come around the corner from the kitchen, "Annie, come get your dog!" She heard her mother scream. Annie flew down the stairs and caught up to Molly. She snatched her up and proceeded back up the stairs to finish with her bath. "Uncle Jack said you were not a fan of baths, but Molly, did you have to jump out of the tub on me?"

Annie was out of breath when she reached the top of the stairs. She sat Molly back down into the tub; only this time, she held her rear end in place with one hand while using the other hand to scrub her fur. Annie sang a bath time song to her that she remembered as a child, "Rubber Ducky, you're the one, you make bath time so much fun, Rubber Ducky, Rubber Ducky," she couldn't help but laugh at herself. Molly did finally settle down and let her finish scrubbing her fur from top to bottom. Annie knew Molly had had enough when she looked up at Annie with her big brown eyes as if pleading to be done with this bath. Annie gave in, "You win, Molly, let's get you out of the bath and get you ready for our big day." Annie debated using the hairdryer for drying Molly's fur, even though her Uncle Jack had strongly suggested it in his excellent book of instructions, she decided, just this one time, she was going to skip it.

Annie walked back to her bedroom; Molly followed behind her, jumped up on Annie's bed and began rolling around and shaking her body to get the excess water off her. "Molly, get off that bed now!" Annie screamed out loud. Molly ignored her. She was too busy rolling around and burrowing herself under the bed covers that Annie had just made. Annie jumped up on the bed to meet her face to face, giving her a gentle but firm push. Molly tumbled to the floor. Annie hopped off the bed and walked over to her, "I am not Uncle Jack, and I refuse to let you walk all over me." Molly turned away from Annie's voice, and her head was now facing the wall. Annie couldn't help but laugh, "you really do know how to lighten a mood, don't you, Molly?"

Annie gathered things for her own shower and headed for the bathroom. A quick clean up, she thought as she stepped in the tub. Annie was running behind and hurried as quickly as she could. She thought she had left Molly in the bedroom, but Molly sat on the bath mat when she stepped out of the shower, waiting patiently for her. Annie chuckled. Molly had a lot adjusting. She patted Molly on the head, and they trotted back to the bedroom to finish getting ready for their visit to the Animal Sanctuary.

Annie opened Molly's colossal suitcase. She laid out a few outfits on the bed and couldn't help but giggle at what she saw. Molly had everything, including hoodies, with the word "Diva" sewn across them. She had short-sleeved, long-sleeved shirts, and cute little dresses with matching booties. Most of them were either pink, purple, or camo pink. There were a raincoat and rain boots for rainy days. She even had several pairs of jammies that Annie was not aware of until this morning. *She wondered if Molly felt chilly last night without the added layer.*

Annie opened up the side pouch and found several hats and tiaras and couldn't help but laugh again. *She had a lot to learn about taking care of this little one.* Annie picked out Molly's outfit for the day. She went with a short sleeve dress. A pink and white striped dress with white letters on the back, "my daddy loves me." Annie grabbed some treaded booties that matched the pup's dress. A matching bonnet to shield her eyes from the sun and Molly was ready. Luckily, Molly was used to wearing clothes, so getting her dressed went quickly. Annie's attire for the day was a little less extravagant. A pair of jeans, tank top, over-jacket, and some sandals, and she was ready. Yes, they were high heel sandals, but when she had packed, she had not planned for a visit to a dirty rundown sanctuary.

CHAPTER 5

Annie And Molly Tour the Animal Sanctuary

Annie grabbed Molly and ran down the stairs; her mom and dad were already in the car: waiting. Annie hopped in the back seat while holding onto Molly as if she were a child. Thankfully, it was just a short drive down the road and around the corner. Annie's mom had already begun sneezing. Annie hadn't been down that road in years, but it was clear to her that her parents had. They were hiding something, but Annie wasn't sure what?

Just as Annie's dad pulled his car around the corner, she saw it. – the property her Uncle Jack had left her: Annie's eyes grew wide. "You have to be joking!" Annie yelled out loud. "It has potential." her dad said as he turned to look at the expression on Annie's face. "You knew this all along, dad; this place is a dump," Annie yelled. "Why didn't you tell me before wasting my time coming out here?"

The house was a typical two-story farmhouse with a wrap-around porch. The shutters were probably a beautiful accent at one time, but now most of them were either falling off or needing some good old-fashioned elbow grease and paint. She was sure there had been a walkway at one time, but now the only thing visible was an outline of one.

Well, if you would just calm down, we can get out of the car, and take a look at the land," barked Annie's father. "It is an excellent piece of property. You need to look beyond the rundown outbuildings, the unkempt fields, and the weathered shutters. The house just needs a little love, and it would make the perfect home."

Annie was about to lose her mind. But at her father's request, she and Molly got out of the car to look around. The walkway was less than visible, and it was apparent that no one had been to visit this house in years. She kicked back the Bermuda grass that covered the walkway.

Annie grabbed ahold of Molly's leash. The last thing she wanted was to have Molly run off. There was no telling what would be hiding in those run-down abandoned buildings.

"Dad, this place is a dump. I don't know why you insisted on us coming here. I have no intention of fixing it up or moving here. Inheriting Molly is plenty to handle," She shouted! Annie immediately apologized to Molly for saying such harsh words about her, but if she were honest: it was the truth.

Annie knew Molly was going to have a hard time adjusting to New York, and likewise for her. Annie had never owned a dog, let alone to be living in a city apartment with no access to the outdoors without riding an elevator or worse yet the stairs, every time Molly would need to do her business.

Annie's dad ignored her comments and continued to walk

toward the house. He insisted that with, some tender loving care, this would make a fantastic home and an excellent business. Annie noticed the smirk on her dad's face, and for some reason, she was immediately annoyed.

"Do you have the key, Annie? I would like to go in and check it out!" yelled Annie's dad from the porch.

Annie picked up her pace and climbed the stairs to the wrap-around porch taking a deep breath when she arrived at the top. The sun was shining. She had to admit to herself that the view was simply amazing, although she would never admit that out loud. Molly seemed to approve, as well. Her tail wagged as Annie reached into her pocket for the key and handed it to her father. Within seconds they were inside the old house. It felt as though they were entering another era. The foyer was huge, with double doors that adorned stained glass windows. The hardwood floors were in good condition, with a little sanding, and polishing they would look as good as new.

Annie was shocked at how well- maintained the interior remained. She and Molly wandered from room to room. There were so many rooms to go through. They kept roaming from room to room, eventually coming back to where they had started. The kitchen left much to desire. The house was going to require a lot of work, that is of course if she decided to stay. Annie made the mistake of using those words aloud, and her dad just smiled. He knew once she took a walk around inside this old house, she was going to fall in love. Paintings still hung on the walls. One, in particular, stood out. It was a picture of a little boy holding a pup in his arms. He looked to be no more than five or six years old, and the puppy appeared to be a lot for him to handle. Annie smiled at the picture. A new frame and some dusting off, she thought she might keep it right where it was. *It would be fun to find out who this young man was, especially if he was going to be hanging in my office. Did I refer to this as my office?* She laughed at the thought.

Annie heard someone call out to her from the front door. It was her mom. "Annie, I never thought, for one minute you would be willing to take a look at this place, that is why I waited in the car." Annie smiled. "This place has a lot of character," said Annie's mom. "I used to visit Mr. and Mrs. Young when I was a young woman. Mrs. Young used to keep an eye on you and your brother when I was in a pinch for a sitter. I am surprised you don't remember being here? Their son James was just a little older than you, but he never attended public schools. He was home-schooled when he was a young boy. He later attended private schools when he became too for his mother to teach. Mr. and Mrs. Young had seven children. James was the youngest child. I never knew the older kids very well. I know they lost a daughter, that was two years older than James, to a farm accident, one summer. No one ever talked about it, but I know Mrs. Young suffered much depression over it.

"What a sad story, said Annie. "I would love to find out the history of this house. I wonder how long it had been an animal sanctuary, what happened to all of the children, and why the house was just left abandoned?" Annie's dad poked his head around the corner. "Well, Annie, if you stick around, I am sure we can find out all of those answers to your questions."

Annie didn't respond but instead ran up the stairs. She couldn't wait to see how those rooms looked. She didn't want to admit it, especially to herself, but she was falling in love with the place. Although her dad was right that it needed some handy work, she loved everything about the old house. She loved the way the big windows allowed the sunshine to come through, the hardwood floors, and the spiral staircase that was worn but not without character. Annie counted the bedrooms as she made her way down the hall. One, two, three, four. She kept going because there was a room at the end of the hallway that she could see from the top of the stairs. For some reason, this was the room that called to her. She stepped inside the room, and immediately felt the sunshine from the windows warming her face and her shoulders. There were three large windows: one overlooking the fields. She could see for miles. There was a pond, on the premises, that she was not aware existed. If there was one thing Annie loved: it was exploring.

Just like a little kid, she flew down the stairs with Molly in tow. "Dad!" she screamed! "There is a pond, in the backfield, have you ever been to see it?" Annie's dad caught off guard. "I have not been to see it, but I am free right now if you want to take a walk down there?" Annie looked down at her shoes. High heels on an adventure like this wasn't her best idea, but she knew without a question she had to go exploring.

Annie's mom was content to stay in the house and look around. If she got bored of doing that, she could always sit on the steps of the wrap around a porch. It was a lovely day, and the views here were spectacular.

Annie was so excited. She felt like a little kid in a candy shop. There was so much to explore. The old place no longer felt like a dirty- abandoned sanctuary. It felt like a home with a need for some TLC.

Her excitement left her rather abruptly when she thought about Sam. *How could she ever leave Sam or their apartment that she has called home for so many years? New York was her home, and Sam was her very best friend in the whole world.*

Annie's dad was already ahead of her, and Molly. "Come on!" he yelled.

Annie thought her dad was even more excited than she was. She walked quickly past the buildings. She planned on checking them out more, on the way back. Right now, her excitement was focused, on seeing the pond, so she continued her trek there. She picked up Molly as she struggled walking through the tall weeds. Molly was just too short to make her way through. Annie spotted her dad just a few feet ahead. He was standing at what appeared to be a dock that was at the base of the pond. Annie's eyes grew big. It was the biggest pond she had ever seen.

"Is this a man-made pond?" she asked her dad. He just shrugged; apparently, he had no idea either, but it was massive. "I could put a canoe in this pond," said Annie. "Well, that is if I decide to stay. There is just so much to think about right now, and I am still not sure that staying here is the right thing to do."

"Let's go take a look at some of these outbuildings," said Annie's dad. He was disappointed that Annie was even considering leaving after how excited she had been. He led the way, and Annie, still carrying Molly, followed. There were five outbuildings: total. Annie didn't know much about animal sanctuaries, but she figured she could google it and find out what she wanted to know. Annie followed her dad into the first building they had come to. It was the farthest from the house and appeared to be the largest. He opened the big barn doors, and right at that moment, a flock of birds flew out. "Sorry for disturbing you!" Annie shouted.

The building was huge but appeared to be empty. Annie

wasn't sure if this farm was ever an animal sanctuary or if this was just one of her Uncle Jack's great ideas to get her to return to her hometown. The building was in structurally sound shape except for the weeds growing around it and a few busted out windows. Although Annie would not admit it, she was assessing the numbers in her head. *How much would it cost? How useful would it be?* Annie was not used to having a lot of money. Uncle Jack left her a lump sum of three hundred thousand dollars, but she wasn't sure she wanted to blow it all: fixing this place. Annie followed her dad through the rest of the buildings. They all seemed to be structurally sound, with just a few minor repairs needed.

Annie and her dad thought they had been through all of the outbuildings until they heard a sound. Even Molly heard it while lying in Annie's arms, half asleep. She perked up her head and looked around. Molly gave a little bark. Annie and her dad heard the sound again. There was no point in letting Molly down. First of all, they didn't know what the noise was or where it was coming from; secondly, the weeds were just too ferocious and were attacking Molly's face with her every move. Annie and her dad moved in the direction of the noise. "It sounds like a baby," whispered Annie.

Annie and her dad began to tiptoe and move as quietly as they could through the bushes. The noise was coming from the other side of the house. She spotted what appeared to be an old chicken coop. They moved quickly but quietly towards the coop. The old fence was broken and there were weeds growing through it. Annie's dad took a peek inside the coup. He waved his hand, beckoning Annie to come inside and see what he had stumbled upon. It was a tiny kitten: a black and white kitten with the bluest eyes.

Annie whispered to the kitten. "Everything is going to be okay, kitty, my dad is going to take good care of you, and he will get you out of here. Won't you, dad?" The kitten looked up at the sound of Annie's voice, but it didn't make a sound. Annie's dad avoided her question. He looked around to see if there was a mother cat or any other kittens, but sadly this little one was here all alone.

"This kitten has been here for at least a few days with no food or water. I am not even sure if that is the worst of it. It looks as though the kitten's paw was injured, but I will do my best to get him out of here and get him to a vet," said Annie's dad. Annie's heart sank. She could see the outline of the kitten's tiny rib cage. She knew if they didn't move quickly, this little one was not going to survive. She ran back to the house to get some kind of tool so that her dad could free the kitten. Annie searched every drawer in the house and finally spotted a pair of rusty pliers. These will have to do, she mumbled to herself. She found a small bowl in the cupboard, and filled it some of her bottled water. Annie had no idea how long it had been here or if it was even going to survive. Annie knew her dad, and she knew he would do everything in his power to save this kitten. Annie's heart began to race; she hadn't felt this alive or needed in years.

Annie ran down the back-porch steps, practically leaping off the bottom one. She ran as fast as her legs would allow. Thankfully her dad had kept Molly with him; otherwise, it would have taken her that much longer.

Annie quickly handed her dad the pliers and watched how he masterfully separated the wires, and he was able to free the kitten.

"This is just half the battle," said Annie's dad. "He has been injured. We don't know how long he has been here. He has not eaten in a very long time, as you can tell from his frail little body. My friend Joe is a vet in town, and hopefully, he will be able to help."

Annie and her dad raced back to the house. Her mom was still on the porch and saw them running toward her. Before she could even ask any questions, Annie motioned for her to get in the car. Annie's mom didn't hesitate and waited until they were inside of the vehicle to ask questions.

"What is going on?" asked Annie's mom. "I saw you both racing toward the car. Where did that kitten come from? Is it going to be okay? Where are we taking it?"

Annie's dad sat in silence while driving. Annie shared as many details as she could, although she didn't know much. They came upon a kitten stuck in the chicken coup. "He was injured, and we are now taking him to some guy by the name of Joe, who is a local vet.

Annie Meets Joe, the Local Vet

Annie's dad pulled up in front of the Veterinarian's office or, as he referred to it, "Joe's place." She handed Molly off to her mom, in the front seat, before stepping out with the kitten. Luckily, her dad joined her. He and the vet were good friends. He held the screen door as she opened the inner wooden door that led to the receptionist's area. Annie looked around. The furniture was clean even though it showed signs of wear. The waiting room consisted of six black-padded metal chairs in front of a large bay window that allowed the sunshine to enter the room. There were real-life photos, with captions of dogs and cats and several Thank You cards placed sporadically on the wall. Her eyes gazed upon the walls of the small room, she spotted a picture of a young man holding up an award; she walked closer to it; he was handsome and young. She wondered if this was a picture of the vet she was about to meet. She read the document, and it was definitely a veterinarian award, in honor of Joe Davis, given on December 8, 2017. Annie tried to read the rest of the document but was distracted when she heard the phone's click.

"May I help you?" the raspy-voiced older woman asked. Seconds later, the woman spotted Annie's dad and ran out from behind the desk. "Ben!" she shrieked with a big smile on her face. "What brings you here? I haven't seen you in years. If I recall correctly, your wife was allergic to all animal hair, so you never had any pets of your own, such a shame." she said with a bit of sarcasm. "Animals are angels sent to us from heaven, and it's up to us to take care of them, isn't that right, Ben?"

Annie interrupted. "My Uncle Jack would often say that all while I was growing up. He would have liked you."

"What brings you in here today on such a beautiful afternoon?" Florence, the receptionist, asked.

"We are here to see Joe. We found a kitten on some property we were looking at, and the poor little thing is in bad shape. We were hoping to see Joe, is he here?" Annie's father asked.

Before Florence could answer, Annie caught a glimpse of a rather tall man dancing his way down the hall. His voice was uplifting as he belted out a tune that Annie did not recognize. Annie chuckled when the young man had to slouch through the archway, to make his way into the room where they had been waiting. Annie could feel her heart racing. She wondered if this was Joe. The guy, her dad, had talked on and on about on the ride over. Annie's heart was racing, she tried to look away, but the rhythm of his walk captivated her eyes. He was incredibly handsome. His dark hair dancing with his big brown eyes, his body was lean yet muscular, and he moved in such a way that made it impossible for Annie to look away.

"Ben!" the young man shouted. "My friend, what brings you here on such a lovely afternoon?"

Before Annie's dad could speak, Joe spun around and looked at Annie. "And more importantly, who is this lovely woman standing at your side? She is too young to be your mistress," he said with a smile.

Annie blushed. She was looking forward to the introduction. She immediately felt the sweat building up in the palm of her hands. Joe stuck out his hand for a formal greeting, "I am Annie" she stammered.

"Hi Annie, I am Joe. I have heard so much about you over the years. The last I knew; you had moved to the big city and had no use for the common folk around here." Annie didn't know how to respond to that comment. She wasn't sure if he was being sarcastic, but she found herself a little irritated by the statement. *Handsome Joe could work on his people skills a little.*

Annie's dad stepped between them. If he knew anything, he knew his little girl was struggling to keep her mouth shut. "Well, Joe, as I was telling Florence, we found this kitten on some property we were looking at this morning. It looks as though it found itself trapped and had been there for a few days. I was able to free it, but I'm afraid it may have some internal damage, and with it being so frail, I thought you would be its best chance for survival."

"Dad, this could take a while. Would you mind taking Mom and Molly back to the house? I am sure mom's allergies are full-blown by now, and Molly needs her lunch. Her food is in the cupboard by the fridge. I'll call you when we are finished." Annie's dad nodded. He knew his wife Rose was trying to be a good sport, but he was sure that her allergies were most likely at their peak by now. It would be a good idea to get them both back to the house and separated.

Joe smiled. "Come on, Annie, let's take this little kitten in the back room, and we'll see if we can fix it up." Annie followed behind him gently holding the kitten in her arms. "Any idea if it's a male or female or who it might belong to," he asked?

Florence ran down the hall after them. "There was a little boy and his mother in here a few days ago. They said they had lost their kitten and wanted to know if I had heard or seen anything. The mother had explained how they had been wandering around Young's farm the other day with the family, and Chad insisted on bringing his new kitten with them. The mother said when they were ready to leave, they were unable to locate the kitten."

Annie spoke up. "You should know that what you referred to as the Young's Farm, that property is actually up for sale. I might add that it is private property. They can't just go wandering on other people's property without permission." Florence didn't know what to say, so she turned around and walked back toward the receptionist's desk, yelling behind her, "I'll give the mother a call about the kitten!"

Annie and Joe continued to walk back down the hallway. Annie could feel the energy from his hand as he swung it back and forth. *What was it about this man?* He ushered her into the small exam room and proceeded to take the kitten from her arms. Annie had wrapped it, in her jacket, and it had laid there motionless for all of this time. Joe placed his hand around the kitten and scooped him away. Annie was shocked at how masculine yet manicured his hands were.

The moment he laid the kitten on the exam table, Joe knew

this wasn't going to be a quick fix. "Annie," he said, this isn't going to be a quick fix. This little guy, yes, he is a male. He's going to require surgery. I can't do that until tomorrow morning when our anesthesiologist comes in. She only works mornings, and she has already left for the day. I will stitch up what I can and make him comfortable for the evening, but there isn't anything more that we can do for him tonight."

"You have been so helpful, Joe. I'll call my dad for a ride now," she said, *half hoping that he would offer to take her back to her parent's home.*

Before she had a chance to dial the phone, Joe spoke up. "Please, Annie, let me take you home. Your father and I have been friends for years, and he has helped me out on more occasions than I can count." Annie nodded. She tried to remain calm and not let him see the excitement running through her entire body. *Who was this man, and why was he having such a effect on her?*

Joe yelled to Florence that he was taking Annie home as they walked out the back door and into the private parking lot. Joe pointed to the black Yukon at the end of the lot. Annie was not the least bit surprised by his taste in vehicles as he walked her to the passenger side and opened the door. Annie laughed as she held the bar to hoist herself into the car. "You probably needed a big enough vehicle so you won't have to duck to get in," she said. Joe smiled; "You're not the first person to say that to me, Annie." He reached in to hand her the shoulder belt. Annie watched him as he walked around to the other side of the truck. He walked with such confidence and pride; his hands swayed from side to side as if in a slow-motion film. Joe smiled at her through the window. *He really is a magnificent creature.*

———

CHAPTER 7

Annie Gives Sam the Brush Off

Annie was quiet on the drive to her parent's house. She was in a comfortable spot right now. She just wanted to enjoy the view: inside and out. Joe continued with the small talk as he drove. "Annie, I am curious; how long do you plan to stay in Murphy?"

She shrugged, "I haven't figured that out yet. As you know, I am back in town because my Uncle passed away. I flew out here to attend his services. Today we went and looked at some property that he had left for me in his Will."

Joe was curious, "Do you mean the property where you found the kitten?"

"Yes, the Young's old piece of property, that is where we found the kitten. It is a large piece of land with an old farm house that is in need of some work, but it still has a lot of potential.

Joe turned his head away from the road and looked directly into her eyes: "What do you want to do, Annie?"

Annie didn't know how to respond to the very question she asked herself for days now. "I don't know," was all that came to her mind.

Joe pulled off the road and down the driveway; Annie was disappointed that they arrived at the house so quickly. He didn't ask to come in. He could tell that she had had a long day. Annie thanked him for everything and told him she would see him later. He drove off, and Annie watched as the truck lights slowly disappeared down the road.

Up to this point, this trip has been a whirlwind, now more than ever; she was missing Sam and their apartment. She thought she could see herself living here, but could she? She gave up this town once: for a reason. *Did it make sense to risk losing everything she had in New York to move to a town and a life she wasn't sure she wanted?* Annie tried to shake off the feelings of anger and sadness. She was angry at Uncle Jack for putting her in this situation and sad that she never got to say goodbye. She strolled up the walkway and entered the house. Annie's thoughts were interrupted when Molly came running down the stairs. She was running as if she were on fire. Her tongue was hanging out, and her smile was the biggest Annie had ever seen. *Dogs do smile, don't they?*

Annie snatched up Molly... "Did papa feed you?" She asked. "I fed Molly, and we even shared a few snacks, didn't we Molly?" she heard him snicker from the kitchen.

Annie walked with Molly in her arms, as they headed toward the kitchen. She sat down, and when she did, she sighed heavily. The day took its toll, and she was exhausted; Annie's mom reached out and patted her on the head. "Would you like something to drink, Annie? I have some freshly made tea in the refrigerator?" Annie nodded her head as she went on to tell her mom about the ordeal with the kitten and how she found herself very attracted to Joe. Her mom smiled. Annie had forgotten how uncomfortable it was to have conversations with her mom. It made her feel like a teenager again, in an odd way.

Annie and her mom chatted for a while. Molly laid perfectly still in her lap. Annie felt the warmth of her body and her breath on her hand as she breathed. Annie loved Molly. In just a few short days, she wasn't sure how this little girl had stolen her heart, but it happened—Annie's heart was full whenever she was around Molly. The fear of being her momma was starting to subside, and Annie was developing a routine. She was all Molly had: now that Uncle Jack was gone. Annie wondered how much Molly missed him, and if Molly felt sad inside. She thought Molly looked sad now and then, but she couldn't be sure.

Annie heard a man's voice as he was coming through the front door. She was startled for a moment. The voice sounded just like her Uncle Jack's. Molly's ears perked up, and she listened. Her tail began to wag, and she jumped off Annie's lap with such excitement: heading straight toward the front door. Annie's heart sank. *Did Molly think this was her daddy?* Annie went to retrieve Molly. She knew it was her brother Brian. She hadn't realized just how much her brother's voice sounded like her Uncle Jack's. *It should have been enough that his resemblance to him was surreal, but his voice too?* Brian's resemblance to him brought up all kinds of emotions. Parts of her wanted to laugh, but there were also parts of her that wanted to cry. Annie was still trying to process the death of her favorite Uncle.

The memories she had of him had been buried a long time ago: when she moved away. Being home and seeing Brian, his apparent twin, brought all those feelings to the surface again. She tried to shrug off the emotions, and she smiled when she saw how happy Molly was to see Brian again.

Molly seemed to enjoy the fact that Brian was the spitting image of Uncle Jack. She was already in his arms, licking him all over his face. Brian laughed. He pulled her away to get a good look at her. "Hey sis, is Molly one of those designer dogs? And is there a reason you have this little girl dressed for the runway?" he giggled. "I mean, what's with the outfit?"

Annie chuckled. "Well, Brian, this is the way Uncle Jack took care of Molly, yours truly. She has two suitcases upstairs packed with more clothes than I have with me. I'll have to show them to you later. That reminds me that I am only here until Friday, and I wondered if you would take a ride to Uncle Jack's farm with me? I'll give Aunt Alice a call in the morning."

Annie's mom was coming through the doorway when she heard Annie's comment. "Annie, I thought you had decided to stay here and rebuild the Animal Sanctuary. I thought you fell in love with the place, and what about Molly and Joe?"

Brian lifted his eyebrow, "Joe, Joe, the vet? Annie, we need to talk more." he said, with a smirk on his face.

Annie felt pressured and was aggravated that people were making her feel that way. "This trip has been exhausting, Mom!" yelled Annie in a much louder voice than she had intended. "You don't understand, I have a life in New York, and I love my life. I have Sam and a beautiful apartment. I love my job. I am not sure that I want to give all of that up to live on a farm. "Mom, look at me, I am not a farm girl.?" Annie held out her foot, showing her very expensive high heeled sandal now covered in mud. Before Annie's mom could respond, Annie snatched Molly from Brian's arms and ran up the stairs to her room. She needed some time to be alone, some time to think. She took off her shoes one by one: assessing the damage. These were her favorite sandals. She had treated herself to them last year for her birthday. Molly jumped up on the bed to greet her. Annie snuggled up to Molly rubbing her belly while trying to soothe away her own frustration. Moments later, her cell phone rang. Annie looked and saw it was Sam. She wasn't sure if she wanted to answer the phone or not but decided at the last minute to answer the phone before he hung up.

"Annie? Are you okay?" she heard Sam's voice on the other end. "I have been trying to call you all day." I know you have a lot going on right now, but I wanted to share some exciting news with you. "Do you remember the project I was telling you about at work?"

Annie had to think about it, she was a little embarrassed to admit it for a moment, but most of his work had to with research and data analysis. She never understood most of it.

"Yeah, yeah, sure," she said. "How is that going?"

"Annie, they gave me a promotion! Sam shouted.

Annie could hear the excitement in Sam's voice. She didn't know what to say. After a very long pause, she whispered, as if in a robotic state, "congratulations."

Sam was disappointed by her response, and she knew it. She wanted to be more excited for him. She knew that he had worked long hours and weekends to get this project off the ground. Annie was barely listening to Sam's voice as he rattled on about his project and promotion. Sam could tell by her lack of enthusiasm that his best friend had no interest in what he was saying. Sam apologized for interrupting her evening and told her he would talk to her in the morning. Annie's mind was still reeling from the day's events, and without even saying goodbye, she hung up the phone. Annie felt terrible for Sam; she should have been more excited for him. He shared what he thought was fantastic news, and all she could muster was a generic congratulations. Annie promised herself she would call him in the morning and apologize, but for now, she just wanted to rest.

Annie pulled Molly closer to her; she loved the feeling of her soft fur next to her skin. *Oh, Annie, what is happening to you?* She thought to herself. Within minutes, Annie drifted off. She dreamt of her Uncle Jack's farm and how excited she would be when he would come to pick her up. She imagined him pulling up to the house in his red pickup truck, the same truck he always drove when he came out to the house, he would roll down his window, and with a big smile on his face, wave for her to get in the truck.

A loud noise awakened Annie. It took her a moment to figure out what the noise was, and she laughed when she realized it was Molly snoring. She had never heard a dog snore before. *This little girl's snore sounded just like a human snore, a very loud human snore.*

Annie rolled over and looked at her phone that had been charging on the stand. The time on her phone read four o'clock. She found it hard to believe she had been asleep for two and a half hours. She rolled out her of the bed. She skipped the mud-covered, high-heeled sandals, opting to walk barefooted for now. She grabbed Molly and ran down the stairs. She knew she should probably let her walk a little more often, or this would become her norm, and Annie didn't want to be carrying her everywhere they went.

CHAPTER 8

Annie's Mom Invites Guests for Dinner

"I am in the living room, Annie. Your mother has gone to the store for a few groceries; She made some cookies and put them in the refrigerator." Annie's dad called out.

Annie walked into the kitchen. She wasn't sure if she wanted to eat, but she knew Molly must be starving. Annie was thankful that her Uncle had prepared some of Molly's food ahead of time and that there were still a few meals left in the freezer. According to him, Molly had never eaten store-bought food, and Annie wasn't sure what it would do to her stomach if she tried now. She grabbed Molly's dinner out of the freezer and warmed it in the microwave. "Here you go, little girl, I know you must be starving," Annie giggled.

Molly never turned away food. Every time she would eat, it was in a devouring motion; this time was no different. If it hadn't been for the instructions of Molly's eating schedule, if Annie didn't know better, she would have thought she was starving.

Annie's mind wandered off again. *Who was going to look after Molly while she was at work? Who was going to let her out during the day and take her for walks? Sam often worked late, and with his promotion, she assumed he would be working even longer hours. Schedules would have to change to accommodate Molly, right?*

Annie's thoughts were interrupted when her mom came through the back door carrying several bags of groceries. Annie rushed over to help her. She grabbed the bags from her mother's hands and set them on the counter. Annie was surprised at how out of breath her mom had become just carrying a few grocery bags. She hadn't thought about the fact that her mom and dad were getting up there in years. Annie tried to recall the last birthday party she had attended. It was four years ago, and it was for her mother's sixtieth party.

"Are you okay, mom?" Annie asked. Her mom waved her hand at her as if to dismiss the question.

"Annie, I have invited some of our friends over tonight for dinner. Helen has been in bad health, and we thought she could use a night out of the house. We also invited her husband and their son Gherk. Your dad has offered to cook steaks on the grill, are you okay with that?" her mom asked. Annie nodded, "sure, mom, sounds good."

She remembered Helen and her family from years ago. Annie also remembered their son, Gherk. At that moment, she realized she didn't even know his birth name. She wondered where he got the nickname. He was older than Annie and was a few years ahead of her in school. She didn't know if he would remember her. He, on the other hand, wasn't easily forgotten. He was the local football star at the high school they attended. Annie remembered the way Gherk couldn't walk down a hallway of their school without being noticed. The girls would stand on the sidelines at his games to get one quick look from the super jock. Annie didn't know why, but she was never interested. Besides, it was not very often Gherk would find himself single; he would move from dating one cheerleader to dating the next.

Annie's mind skipped back to the moment her mom said they were all coming for dinner, and she felt her stomach twinge. Annie turned, looked at her mother, and said, "please, please tell me you are not going to try to fix me up with Gherk?" Annie's mom smiled. "Of course, not dear."

Annie wasn't hungry, but she decided she would hang around and socialize for a little while. She didn't want her mom's guests to think of her as being rude. Although Annie was never a fan of small talk or small social gatherings with people she barely knew, she decided tonight she would make an exception.

Annie had only been away from New York for a few days, and she already found herself missing so many things about her life there. She loved being part of a big city and loved being part of the fast pace. It made her feel alive inside. She loved that she could live next door to someone and not know their name or personal business. She loved the crowds of people who would gather to listen to a local band at one of the parks, the smell of bakeries and restaurants as she walked down the street, and food delivered right to her door. She chuckled when she thought about the conversation, she had with her mom the other night.

Annie had asked her mom, "Where is the best place to

order pizza from, and if they delivered?" Annie's mom laughed and shook her head no.

"How about Chinese food?" Annie said, waiting for her mother's facial expression. Her mom shook her head no again.

"Okay, mom, I know this one is a reach. How about Grub Hub?" Annie asked. Again, Annie's mom shook her head no, and they both laughed.

Annie's dad interrupted her thoughts as he came walking into the kitchen with Molly trotting behind him. She felt another tinge of guilt. She had gotten so caught up in her own thoughts – she hadn't noticed that Molly had wandered off.

"Molly, were you keeping papa company?" Annie said. Annie was relieved by the expression on her dad's face. He enjoyed Molly's company.

"Molly and I will go hang out in the living room. Call me when it's time to light the grill." Said Annie's dad as he picked up Molly and walked away.

Annie helped her mom prep for dinner. She knew it wouldn't be long before everyone arrived, and her mother wanted to have everything prepared ahead of time. A few moments later, her guests arrived. Helen was the first one to walk through the door. Annie reached out to give her a kiss and hug. She was surprised at how frail Helen looked, and how much she had aged. Sydney, with his hand in the middle of her back, followed closely behind her. It was a nice gesture, and Annie was sure that was at least in part to keep her from falling. Gherk was sure to make a grand entrance, true to form. Annie wondered if his confidence was more of a show than his true feelings – he had always appeared so confident. Annie watched as he undressed her with his eyes.

Then it happened. Gherk swung open his arms and lifted her in the air as if she were twelve again. Annie didn't know what to do or say, so she just went with it. Annie wasn't sure why grown men thought she would enjoy being tossed around like she was a ragdoll, but in this case, she didn't mind. She was enjoying the attention.

"Let me get a good look at you, big city girl!" he laughed. "You haven't changed a bit. You always were a gorgeous gal, Annie, and I would have loved to have dated you."

Annie found herself speechless, it didn't happen very often, but he managed to render her that way. Her mind raced with so many different responses she could have made to that comment, but none seemed appropriate. She glanced up at him as he sat her down. *There must be something in the Texas water that makes these men grow so tall,* she thought. It was no surprise that Gherk had been a football star all through high school. He stood at least six feet- two and from what she could tell, and he was still solid as a rock. He was a good-looking man with his blue eyes and blond hair. Annie just never found herself attracted to him, perhaps because of his cocky attitude.

Annie's mom interrupted and waved them all to the patio area. It was a beautiful Texas evening. The sun had gone down, and the temperature was mid-seventies. If there was anything Annie missed about living in Texas, it was the weather. New York undoubtedly had its share of severe weather. Sometimes it would even snow, Annie shivered at the thought. It was the perfect evening. They spent a few hours reminiscing and bantering back and forth about the Texan girl living in a big city.

Gherk went on to tell her of his brief marriage to his high school sweetheart. Annie mumbled under her breath; she wasn't sure who that might be. There had been so many. He went on to tell her that it ended in a nasty divorce and custody battle over their four-year-old daughter Emma: a year ago. Annie did the math and noticed that they hadn't wasted any time going from wedding to baby carriage. Gherk explained to her that he had visitation every other weekend, and he would be happy to bring Emma over some time to meet her... Annie could see the love in Gherk's eyes when he spoke of his daughter. The unconditional love he felt for her was written all over his face.

Annie nodded. She wasn't sure if this was his way of being polite or if he was, in fact, interested in her? She dismissed the thought. It was getting late; Annie said her goodbyes and called Molly to follow. When Molly didn't come right away, Annie called her again. It was not like her to ignore Annie's call. Annie looked over in Gherks' direction and giggled. Molly had made a new friend, and he was doing the unthinkable. Molly's face was peeking out from underneath the table. Her mouth was full of the steak that Gherk had so secretly given her. Before Annie could say a word, Helen had already stepped in.

"Eric Sydney Brown!" His mother shouted across the table. "It is not polite to feed someone else's dog just because they're begging for your food. You should have asked for permission first."

"It's okay, Mrs. Brown, said Annie: laughing. "I know first-hand how hard it is to say no to Molly."

Annie chuckled; it was fun watching Gherk get scolded. Now she knew his birth name. She thought back to her high school days and wondered if she had ever heard him called that? If she did, she didn't recall it now. Annie poked fun at him. "I often wondered if Gherk was your birth name," said

Annie. Eric's mom chimed in, "It's a funny story of how Eric got his nickname. When he was born, his sister Elizabeth was only three years old. She had some trouble saying his name, and it always sounded like Gherk. We joked about it at the time, but the name stuck, and here he is almost thirty years old and still goes by Gherk." They all laughed at the story.

"If it's okay with you, I would prefer to call you Eric," said Annie.

Eric nodded. She didn't think he cared one way or another, but it helped her feel less like a high school girl. Annie grabbed Molly and ran up the stairs. It had been a long day and she still needed to reach out to her Aunt Alice for a visit.

Annie pushed the door to her bedroom open and closed it quietly behind her. She loved this space. It was bright and cheery and comforting all at the same time. She quietly reminisced over the few slumber parties she had while growing up. Annie didn't recall having many friends, but she has remained close to the ones she had from childhood. She stretched out on the bed and reached for her phone, where she had left it charging while she sat on the patio. Sam had called three times since Annie talked with him this afternoon. She wasn't sure why sometimes she was missing him not being here, and other times seeing his phone number show up three times on her phone made her angry. Annie decided not to listen to his voicemails and planned to call her Aunt Alice instead. She knew it would be strange visiting her Aunt Alice, knowing her Uncle Jack wouldn't be there.

CHAPTER 9

Annie Makes Her Decision

On the day of her Uncle Jack's service, Annie could only catch up with her Aunt long enough to hug her and offer her condolences. Annie intended to call on Alice the next day to have a more intimate visit with her. Annie wanted to make sure to call her before she left Texas and ask her Aunt if she could be of any help. Before Annie had a chance to dial Alice's phone number, Annie's phone rang, and she picked it up without recognizing the number. It was her Aunt Alice.

Annie had a hard time identifying the voice on the other end of the phone. "Annie, this is your Aunt Alice. I would love you and Brian to visit me at the farm before you head back to New York. Your Uncle Jack has some things here that I think he would have wanted you both to have."

"I have some errands to run in the morning. How does One O'clock sound?" asked Annie. Alice agreed and Annie hung up the phone. She knew Alice loved her Uncle Jack. His death was going to be a difficult time for her. Uncle Jack and

Aunt Alice were high school sweethearts and married right after graduation. Annie knew from past conversations that her Aunt Alice had never lived on her own. Alice left her parents' home, and she and Jack had lived together until the day he passed. Annie knew Alice had received an inheritance after her parents died, allowing them to live a comfortable life.

The next morning Annie and Molly got up and followed their similar routine. Molly was going to stay with Annie's mom and dad while she ran errands. Annie knew her dad enjoyed spending time with Molly and spoiling her. Annie's mom stayed as far away from Molly as possible. Although, Annie noticed that her mother's sneezing had subsided during the time that Molly had been at the house.

With Molly in his arms, Annie's dad walked her to the door. "I respect any decision you make, Annie, but you know that I am hoping you choose to stay in Murphy." Annie didn't have the heart to tell him she had already made her decision. She knew he wasn't going to be happy. Annie patted Molly on the head. "You be good for Papa," she said as she turned around and walked out the door.

Annie had an appointment with Ralph, the lawyer. He needed her decision today. Although she had gone back and forth between keeping the Animal Sanctuary or staying in New York: she had reached a decision. She decided to sell the Sanctuary.

Annie knew there were advantages to staying in Murphy. Her family lived here, and there would be plenty of room for Molly. Annie thought about Joe as well. They were just beginning to know one another. She tried to imagine what it would be like living on the farm and caring for animals that had suffered physical or emotional trauma. She watched the news and read newspapers. She knew, somewhere in the world, these terrible things happened every day. But was Annie equipped to take on such a task? She was having a hard-enough time with Molly. Annie loved Molly more than anything, but she knew there was more to caring for Molly than just her love.

Besides, Annie was already missing her friends in New York. She had met several of them while attending college and have since remained friends. Annie missed her apartment in New York. She missed looking out the window and watching the hustle and bustle on the streets and missed the honking horns, the buses whizzing by her apartment complex. She missed the curbside restaurants, and yes, she even missed take out and grub hub.

Annie walked through the door of the lawyer's office. His secretary greeted her, and the young woman ushered Annie to Ralph's office, where he sat behind the desk in his chair: waiting.

"I trust that since you are here, Annie, you have made your decision?" said Ralph.

Annie nodded. She was hoping it was the right one. It was the hardest decision she has ever made. "Yes, I do need to get back to New York. My job is there, and my boss is already asking when I will return. I want to sign the papers to put it on the market. You can reach me by phone or email when the property sells." said Annie.

Ralph's facial expression said it all, he was disappointed, and in some regard, she was also. But ultimately, it had to be her decision. He quickly spread out the papers for her to sign. Annie felt as though she was signing her life away. The pages just kept on coming, and she kept on signing. Annie was looking forward to getting out of his office, he was no longer his usual chatty self, and the room had now become uncomfortably quiet.

Annie extended her hand when she stood up to say goodbye. He didn't bother to get up from behind the desk. A quick handshake, she thought, and she would be out the door. "Annie, I want you to know I think you are making a huge mistake. I wish you would reconsider. Your Uncle Jack spoke highly of you, and I know you are capable of amazing things. I will hold the paperwork for twenty-four hours before turning into the real estate agency."

Annie nodded but didn't respond to his comment. She was feeling nauseous and wanted to get back to the car. She sat in silence for a few moments before even starting the engine. The sun was shining, and it was another beautiful Texas day. She never grew tired of the weather in Texas.

—◆—

CHAPTER 10

Annie Runs into Joe

Annie looked at the clock on the dashboard. It was only ten-thirty, so she had some to kill. She went in search of a diner or cafe. She wanted to grab a coffee, clear her head, and plan to meet her brother Brian; at the house, around noon. Annie decided there was plenty of time to do so. And more than anything, she wanted to be alone with her thoughts.

She drove around the block to get on the main drag. She was surprised at how many people there were walking around in such a small town. *Where were they all going?* she wondered. She found a small cafe on the corner of the street. It wasn't much to look at — she hoped the inside would be a little more inviting. Annie parked the car and walked inside. The interior of the cafe was much more attractive than the outside. She was thankful for that. There were several dining tables strategically placed to fit as many customers as possible: without feeling crowded. There was a counter large enough to accommodate six additional customers. The décor on the walls was outdated but appealing. There were a few funny signs and some pictures of cacti: not unusual for a Texan diner.

Annie grabbed a seat at the counter. The cafe was busy this Tuesday morning; looking around, she saw it was a mixed crowd, many looked to be retired. She assumed some of the younger folks were college students. Annie sat with her back facing the door. She turned around quickly — startled by the voice coming up from behind her and whispering in her ear.

Annie smiled. "Hi, Joe, what brings you in here this morning?" She looked at Joe's whimsical eyes and how they danced when he saw her. Joe had a charism about him that Annie couldn't deny. She loved his style. His jeans hugged him at every curve, a wide belt buckle that drew her attention to his lean, fit abs. He chuckled. "I could ask you the same thing? I just finished up the surgery on the kitten you brought in," he replied. He did great and is now in recovery. The mother and her young son waited all morning in the waiting room until the surgery was over."

Annie smiled. "I was actually on my way over there to see how the little guy was doing. I just wanted to enjoy a cup of coffee first."

"I am happy to have to run into you today, she said. I'll stop by your office for a quick visit with the kitten. It will be good to see the little guy under better circumstances..." said Annie.

Joe nodded. "Well, I have to get back to the office. I was getting the coffee to go—one for me and one for my receptionist." Annie was glad that he finished his sentence with those words. *She was wondering who the other cup of coffee might belong to? Then she asked herself why she even cared?* Joe leaned in to kiss her on the cheek, and as he did, his hand ever so gently touched the small of her back. Annie felt his hand's electricity run up and down her body, from her head to her toes. It was so intense she was wondering if he could feel it too. She was frightened by this unknown feeling that crept up on her whenever he was around. "*Was this love?* "Anne wondered. She thought she had been in love before, but it never came close to feeling like this. Before Annie could even gather the rest of her thoughts, he disappeared out the door. She finished her coffee and drove over to the vet's office. Annie smiled when she remembered her dad, referring to it as "Joe's Place." *That comment fit,* she thought to herself.

Florence recognized Annie as soon as she walked through the door. "Hi, Annie," she said. "I heard you were on your way over; I'll take you back where Whiskers is recovering."

"Whiskers, huh," asked Annie. "That is a great name for him."

Florence went on to tell her what she already knew, but Annie didn't stop her. It was clear she was excited to tell the story. "Joe is in the other exam room. He had an emergency come in shortly after he returned with our coffees. It happened so fast I didn't get the details, but Joe didn't think it was as severe as the owners made it sound on the phone."

Annie was relieved that Joe was busy. She wasn't sure if she wanted to see him after the moment they shared at the diner. Annie nodded as Florence ushered her to the room that Whiskers was recovering in. Annie walked through the door and spotted the small kitten. He was sleeping peacefully in a makeshift pet bed that probably had housed numerous animals over the years. She walked over to him and whispered, "hi there, little guy, I am so glad that your family found you and you are on your way to recovery. It looks as though our good friend Joe has taken excellent care of you. Florence told me you should be going home in a day or two."

The kitten lifted his head, she thought. Annie heard his purring. It was a soft, soothing purr. She knew it was too soon to pick him up and hold him, but she was happy that he was aware of her being there. Annie sang him one of her short childhood lullabies. She wished him well and walked out the door. Annie walked down the hall, giving a quick wave to Florence, who was on the phone, and out the door, she went.

CHAPTER 11

Annie And Brian Visit Aunt Alice

Annie looked at her watch. She had just enough time to meet Brian at the house so they could go to visit their Aunt Alice. Annie decided against bringing Molly. She knew Molly would be in good hands while they were gone. She wasn't sure how Molly would react to visiting Uncle Jack's farm, especially with him not being there. Annie wasn't sure how she was going to respond, either. She couldn't remember a time when she had been to the farm, and her Uncle Jack wasn't there.

When Annie arrived back at the house, her brother Brian was parked out front and waiting for her. As she pulled her dad's car into the driveway, she could hear Brian honking his horn. Annie waved to him. She wasn't sure why he seemed to be in such a hurry today but, she grabbed her purse and hurried down the driveway.

"Hey, Brian!" Annie said as she lifted her petite frame into the truck.

Brian was less than enthusiastic when he responded. "Hey, sis, can we please make this a quick visit? I plan to meet up with some friends of mine this afternoon, and I am already running late." Annie responded with a nod; she wasn't looking forward to the visit either. She thought to herself a quick hello, some reminiscing, and they would be back on the road.

They made small talk on the ride there. It was the first time Brian and Annie were alone together in years. They talked about Brian's plans after he graduated. Annie talked about her job, the city, and Sam. She was surprised by how fast the hour drive went by. Before she knew it, they were driving down the long driveway, and Annie could see her Aunt Alice in the distance.

Brian pulled up and shut the truck engine off. Annie didn't move. Suddenly, she felt paralyzed. Brian understood her feelings, and he sat with her for a few moments. "Are you okay, sis," he asked? Annie nodded her head. She knew it was time to get out of the car. She could see her Aunt Alice walking toward them at an accelerated pace: with a dog following close behind.

Annie and Brian got out of the car and walked over to greet her. Alice reached out to hug Annie first. Annie thought her Aunt Alice held onto her for a longer time than she felt comfortable, but given the circumstances, she didn't pull away. Alice took ahold of Annie's hands. "Oh, my child, look at you? I always knew you would grow up to be an amazingly-beautiful woman, and here you are even more beautiful than I could have ever imagined." She held onto Annie's hands for a few moments longer and then turned to face Brian.

"I can't believe my eyes!" she hollered. "You look so much like your Uncle Jack! You have grown into quite a handsome young man, Brian. I'll bet you have to fight those girls off you just like your Uncle had to do all of those years."

Annie saw the tears beginning to well up in Alice's eyes. She didn't want to do this today. Before Annie had the chance to change the subject, Brian blurted out, "Aunt Alice, where is the old dog I saw walking up with you?" Annie was thankful for the distraction as Alice turned and faced in the dog's direction.

"Your Uncle Jack had put in an underground electric fence a few years ago, that is why Simba didn't come any farther to greet you. I knew he would want to see Annie," said Alice. Annie's eyes grew wide in horror. He was not the young pup she had left behind years ago. She had watched him walking up the driveway with Alice when they arrived, and he could barely walk.

"The mass on his back was from an inoperable tumor. Due to his age — Joe had advised against surgery." Alice continued the story, but Annie had already bolted in the direction of Simba.

Annie was sick to her stomach; her mind flashed with the memories she had with him. He was her best friend, all while she was growing up. *He knew all her secrets, why hadn't Uncle Jack told me Simba was in such bad of shape? I would have come to see him.* Annie knew that was a lie, but she was trying to convince herself of it, so she didn't feel the amount of guilt that she did this very moment. When Annie walked beyond the electric fence, Simba hobbled slowly to greet her. His tail wagged faster with every step he took. When he finally reached her, Annie put her arms around him and sobbed. She never expected to see him like this. Annie didn't know what she had expected when she thought about it, but this wasn't it.

"I'm so sorry, Simba!" she cried. "I never should have left you. You were my best friend, and I just left you one day and didn't look back. You have probably spent all of this time wondering what you did to make me go away." Annie sobbed harder as she tried to explain to her childhood friend why she left him.

"I went to college, Simba, and I have a great job now. A job that I love. I didn't leave you because I wanted to. You would have never liked New York." she cried as she caressed his back and the lump that protruded from his back. She was hoping the mass didn't feel as bad as it looked. Annie continued to wipe the tears from her face, but it was of no use. The faster she wiped them away, the faster more came. Annie was ashamed of herself. She wondered how she could have been the kind of person to have left Simba and never looked back, but she did and looking at him now. It was going to be something she would regret for the rest of her life.

Alice and Brian caught up to Annie and Simba. Annie tried to wipe the tears away again with her sleeve, hoping they didn't see how badly she had been crying.

Annie didn't realize that Alice had overheard the conversation she was having with Simba. "Tell you what, Annie?" Alice asked in a slightly sarcastic voice. "Would it have mattered? You made your life away from here, Annie. Although your Uncle Jack hoped that you would return to Simba, and yes, even him one day, I knew he was only fooling himself. You were a big city girl once you left here, and I never saw you coming back." Annie didn't know what to say. As harsh as that was to hear, she knew every bit of it was true.

Brian reached out his hand to pull Annie up from the ground, where she had been sitting with her arms around Simba as if this one hug was going to make everything okay, but she didn't care; she continued to hold him as tight as she could. The three of them walked silently back to the house. Alice led them through the back door to the kitchen. She motioned for them to sit down as she grabbed three glasses from the cupboard.

Alice sat down and went on to talk about their Uncle Jack, her husband, the life he lived over the past few years, and of course – his love of Molly.

"How is Molly getting along without Jack?" Alice asked. "Molly loved Jack, and Jack felt the same way about her. Your Uncle Jack thought, leaving Molly in your care would help sway you into taking over the Sanctuary and moving here. Jack also knew Molly would have a hard time living on the farm without him. She would be looking for him every moment of every day. It was painful enough to watch her grieve while we waited for you to arrive. I will admit I sure do miss her, but Jack and I wanted to do what we thought was best for her: and you. I know she is well taken care of, and I would love to visit her one day at your parent's home if that would be okay?" Alice asked. "I half expected Molly to be at my doorstep within a week of you towing her around. She does take some getting used to."

"Annie, Ralph called me an hour or so ago and told me of your decision to sell the Animal Sanctuary," said Alice. "I am not surprised, but I am disappointed. I will be honest with you, Annie. Your Uncle Jack was very close to Molly, and he convinced himself that by leaving her in your care and leaving you the Animal Sanctuary, you would move back. I told him many times I didn't think that was likely, but I guess he just didn't want to admit it."

Annie shrugged because she didn't know what else to say. She knew everything her Aunt was saying was true. Brian sat there staring into the other room, void of all expression, Annie wondered what was going through his mind, but she didn't want to ask. She had a pretty good idea she knew, and Annie was sure she didn't want to hear him say out loud. The three of them spent the rest of the afternoon going through Uncle Jack's memorabilia and sharing stories. There was laughter and some moments of tears, but Annie thought it was a pleasant visit. She couldn't help but wonder if her dislike of her Aunt Alice was unwarranted. She was quite comical at times, and Annie could see just how much she had loved her Uncle Jack. Annie noticed that Aunt Alice was still wearing her wedding ring. Annie knew that it had only been a short time that her Uncle Jack had passed, but it touched Annie's heart to see it remain on her finger.

Annie and Brian said their goodbyes to Alice and walked out the back door. Annie spotted Simba still in the yard and ran over to him, giving him a big hug and a kiss. Annie was sure he remembered her, as he wagged his tail back and forth. "I promise you Simba, I'll be back to see you," she whispered.

Annie ran to catch up to Brian. He seemed to be walking much faster than he did when they arrived there. Annie didn't ask why. She supposed she didn't ask because she was afraid of what he might say. They loaded themselves into the truck and headed back to her parent's house. There was very little traffic, so it made for a more relaxed drive. The ride home was a silent one. Annie sensed from Brian's death stare earlier, he was aware she was selling the Sanctuary, and he was less than happy about it. He finally broke his silence and told Annie she should tell mom and dad about her decision when they got home. Annie nodded. She knew he was right.

CHAPTER 12

Annie Tells Her Parents of Her Decision

When they got home, Annie followed Brian into the house. She was happy to see Molly greeting them at the door. Annie swooped her up and gave her little kisses all over her furry face. Molly didn't mind all the attention she was getting. She was used to a lot of affection and probably wouldn't survive long without it.

"Were you good for Papa?" Annie asked her as if expecting a response.

Annie heard her dad get up from the chair in the living room, as he made his way out to the foyer. "Molly was an angel! We had a lot of fun together, and I can't wait until we can spend more time together," said Annie's dad.

"Dad, I have some news to share with you and mom. I know you aren't going to be happy, so I think we should sit down and discuss it.

Annie's mom was already in the kitchen, so the rest of them went to join her. Even though he already knew exactly how the conversation was going to begin and end, Brian went along. Annie was going to tell her parents that she would be selling the Sanctuary, after all. She would be returning home on Friday because she needed to get back to her work. Brian chuckled to himself. How many times had he sat at this same table for family meetings of his own? He not only knew how it was going to start — he knew what his parents would say to try and sway her to stay. In the end, Annie was a grown woman and was making the best choice for herself.

The conversation went precisely as Brian, and perhaps even Annie predicted. Annie explained to them she was selling, and the many reasons why. The discussion followed by her parents, giving her the many reasons, she should stay, but in the end, Annie was going to do what she thought was best for her and Molly, even if everyone else disagreed. She excused herself from the table. She walked Molly to the back door and put her on the lead to do her business.

Annie realized she hadn't spent any time with Molly today, and she felt terrible about that, but now it was time for a little peace. Annie was tired of talking and tired of thinking. At this point, she was more than ready to go home. Annie retrieved Molly from the lead. She had already wrapped herself around the stump out in the yard and was barking for help. Annie was able to untangle her. She didn't bother setting her back on the floor after carrying her inside. She just stuffed her under her arm and carried her up the stairs.

Annie sat crossed-legged on the bed with Molly's head resting upon her knee. She decided she would give Sam a call. Annie needed someone to pick her from the airport on

Friday and was hoping he would be available. She knew he was incredibly busy having been recently promoted.

Sam answered the phone after only one ring. "Hi, Sam!" said Annie in her perky voice. "Have you missed me?"

Sam chuckled, "Nah, I have already rented your room to a smokin' hot girl in need of a place to sleep. I assured her you wouldn't mind." Sam said in a joking voice. Annie was silent.

Sam laughed out loud, "Annie, I was only teasing you!"

She snapped out of it and giggled. "Oh yes, I know you were only teasing, she said. I am sorry, Sam, I guess I have a lot on my mind. Will you be able to pick me up at the J.F.K. airport on Friday? Molly and I will be coming home."

Sam didn't hesitate to answer, "Of course, I'll be there just let me know what time your flight is going to land."

Annie thanked Sam, saying her goodbyes as she hung up the phone. She was ready to pull the covers over her head and say good riddance to this day. Molly was happy to snuggle her as they both drifted into dreamland.

Annie woke the next morning with the sun shining on her face. She rolled over to look at the clock on the end stand. She blinked when she saw the time: assuming she misread it. "Ten o'clock!" she yelled. "How could we have slept until ten o'clock, Molly?"

Molly just blinked at her. Annie had to laugh at the sight of her in her camo pajamas. It didn't matter how many times she saw Molly dressed in pajamas, dresses, or long shirts. Annie knew she was always going to chuckle about it.

The next few days that went by were uneventful. Annie was thankful for that. Arrangements had been made for Brian to pick her up and take her to the airport Friday morning, it was a direct flight, so it would be less of a hassle, especially now that she had Molly to contend. Annie was nervous for Molly but felt satisfied with the attendant who assured Annie that she would be well taken care of and that she would be able to retrieve Molly as soon as the plane landed. Annie agreed.

CHAPTER 13

Annie And Molly
Return to New York

Brian showed up early Friday morning — earlier than
Annie had planned: she was caught off guard. She raced
around the bedroom, making sure to pack all of Molly's
belongings. Annie was sure Molly's clothes were not cheap
and didn't want to leave any behind. She made one last sweep
of her bedroom before closing the door behind her. Brian
had already packed their belongings in the car, and he was in
the driver's seat: waiting for them. Annie ran down the stairs.
Her mom and dad were waiting at the door to say their goodbyes. She cried as she hugged them; even Molly got in on the
hugs this time. Annie smiled when she heard her dad whisper
to Molly, "Be a good girl for Papa!" Brain waved his hand out
the car window as if to usher them along. Annie was happy to
oblige. She hated goodbyes. She opened the front door and

ran down the stairs with Molly under her arm as usual. She lifted herself into Brian's truck and sat Molly on her lap.

The ride to the airport was a quiet one. Annie didn't know what to say. She was sure Brian had mixed feelings about returning to New York, and she wasn't in the mood to talk about it. She watched her brother as he stared straight ahead at the road. She had really enjoyed the time they had spent together while she was home and hadn't given it much thought, until now, how much she would miss him. Annie took a deep breath. *Time to go home*, she whispered to herself as he drove up to the airport's front, allowing her and Molly to step out. Annie wasn't too concerned about being in a rush since she had given herself plenty of time before their flight was set to leave. Brian helped with her suitcases and walked them to the gate. He said his goodbyes and kissed them both on their foreheads. Molly responded with a wet sloppy kiss that Annie was sure he would wipe off with his sleeve, but surprisingly he didn't.

Annie giggled. "You sure do know how to capture hearts, don't you, Miss Molly?"

Minutes later, Molly was whisked away, and Annie boarded the plane. She sat in her seat, trying to take her mind off the flight. The young flight attendant could recognize Annie's apprehension and asked her if she needed anything before taking off? Annie shook her head no and turned her head to look out the window. She was thankful for the weather today, not a cloud in the sky. She clutched her seat as the plane ascended into the sky. Annie has never been a fan of flying, especially when she was flying alone. Luckily the plane landed safely in New York and earlier than expected.

Annie was thrilled to be back in New York. As she walked down the ramp, she spotted the airline pet handler holding

Molly. Annie picked up her pace to reach them, handing the woman the claim ticket. She was so excited to be reunited with Molly. She hoped Sam would arrive early. Molly didn't seem to be phased by anything going on around her. With Molly in her arms, Annie quickened her pace when she spotted Sam.

"Sam! Sam!" Annie yelled. She was so happy he arrived early. She dreaded the thought of waiting at the airport: especially with Molly.

Sam ran up to Annie. He wrapped his arms around her and gave her a big kiss. "I have missed you so much, Annie. The apartment has not been the same without you. "Sam's eyes moved in the direction of Molly, who was panting faster than ever.

"This must be the famous Molly?" Sam laughed. "Well, Molly, it looks as though you and your outfit are ready for the Big Apple scene!"

Annie chuckled. She had emptied Molly's suitcase earlier that morning, searching for the perfect outfit for her... Annie came across the perfect dress. It was pink, most of Molly's dresses were pink, with diamond studs sporadically placed over the dress. The dress had a sparkle to it, and Annie laughed when she saw it. She didn't stop at just the clothing, no-no this was a special occasion, and she wanted Molly dressed like a star. Annie opened the side compartment of Molly's suitcase that housed all her accessories. She chuckled again. She had seen it all before, but it never stopped being funny. Some pink booties and a tiara complimented Molly's wardrobe.

"Well, it's my pleasure to meet you, Molly. We are going to have so much fun together." said Sam in a laughing voice. Annie had forgotten how much she missed hearing Sam's laugh. He was usually in a good mood and enjoyed making Annie laugh, and she loved that about him.

Sam helped Annie load the suitcases in the car. The ride back to the apartment was enjoyable. He and Annie picked up right where they had left off before her trip.

CHAPTER 14

Annie And Molly Try to Adjust

Upon arriving at their apartment building, Sam unlocked the door and ushered Annie and Molly into the apartment.

"Thank you, Sam. I have missed you," said Annie as she kissed him on the cheek.

Sam threw his arms around Annie and hugged her. She was sure he missed her as she missed being away from him. Sam stepped out the door to retrieve the rest of her luggage that still sat in the hallway.

Annie was so thankful to be home. She sat Molly on the floor and plopped down on the couch. She had every intention of settling in, but she heard Sam shriek before she had a chance. "Molly! You don't go to the bathroom on the floor. You go to the bathroom outside, that is where you do your business!" Molly coward and ran toward Annie. "It is my fault,

Sam, I'll clean it up and take her outside," said Annie. She grabbed the leash and headed for the door.

After a short while, everyone was beginning to settle in. No doubt, bringing Molly back to New York to live in their small apartment was life-changing. Sam was wrapped up in his work. He was recently promoted as Account Executive in his firm, with far more responsibilities than he had previously as the manager. Annie was never sure exactly what Sam did, but she knew he met with clients day and night. He was often on the phone, and with his new position, he put in even longer hours. *No wonder his company loves his so much,* Annie thought to herself. *He has given up his life to accommodate them. He is barely home to eat dinner, let alone sleep.* Annie teased him, calling him a fictional superhero that didn't require food or sleep. Sam would laugh it off, but he knew it was Annie's way of expressing to him her displeasure. Sam knew he worked too much and would often tell himself that he could settle in and enjoy life a little more once he got the promotion. But Annie knew nothing could be farther from the truth.

Annie's days were just as busy, filled with her own responsibilities, including her job. She was still going to the office at least three days a week and she was thankful for the short commute. Her office was in one of the largest buildings on Broadway; in downtown Manhattan, just a few blocks from the apartment. Annie loved the beautiful days when she and Molly could walk to work and not worry about the traffic. Her office was on the fifth floor, and the windows faced the street: it had a fabulous view. She would sometimes find herself mesmerized by the movement of people going in so many different directions. Several of her coworkers had commented on how lucky she was to have such an ample space. Annie agreed. She was thankful that she had her own office, especially now. And although it was small, it was pleasant enough. When she first took over the office a few years ago, she didn't waste any time decorating with her personal touches. She knew she was going to be there a lot and wanted it to feel comfortable. At the time, Annie's boss, who has now since retired, gave her free reign to do anything she wanted to do with the office space. As far as he was concerned, it was hers, and she has been in the same office ever since. She recalled spending that weekend searching for just the right touches to bring the office to life. There was a large desk that faced the door. Annie decided to leave it that way since it made the most sense. She was thankful for the room darkening blinds to keep the sun out on those bright sunny days. She hung a few of her accomplishments, including her framed Bachelor's degree from N.Y.U. She was proud of her degree and was eager to display it. The previous occupant left behind a large rubber tree plant, and it sat in the corner of the office. After careful consideration, Annie decided to keep it. She never had a green thumb, so she was curious to see how long this plant would survive. The one piece of furniture Annie did have replaced was the old multi-colored desk chair. The receptionist had been so kind the day Annie was hired. Annie recalled how she brought her in several office furnishing catalogs that she used to place orders for office supplies, furniture, and accessories. Annie was excited as she flipped through the pages. She came across a large black leather chair. She envisioned how it would look in her new office and how she would look sitting in it. That black leather chair still sits in her office, and Annie loves it as much today as the day she picked it out.

Last but not least was Annie's favorite picture of her and Sam. They had been out hiking with some of their friends, one of them snapped a photo of the two them sitting under a waterfall. They both looked so relaxed with larger than life smiles on both of their faces. It was Annie's favorite photo. She decided to have a framed copy made and sat it on her desk.

Since Molly would be spending some time in the office, Annie made some additional purchases. She stopped at the local pet store, looking for the perfect bed to accommodate Molly while she spent time in the office. She finally came across the ideal one. It was pink with sparkles on it. The inside lined with fur and Annie purchased a matching blanket to sit inside of it. It came in three sizes, so Annie chose the in-between size for Molly. Annie also purchased some toys that would stay at the office. She tried to recall some of Molly's favorite toys at home to replicate some of them. As funny as it seemed, she thought to herself, *Molly did have favorites.* She had a little white lamb with its entire body covered in soft white fur that squeaked when she chewed on it, a rope toy, and of course, her Kong that you could stick treats or peanut butter in. Annie was happy she could locate all of these at their local pet store and then proceeded to walk out with a few new toys for the office and more for the house. Annie was shocked when the cashier rang it up, "that will be one hundred fifteen dollars, ma'am." said the young man at the register as he bagged up her purchase. Annie was shocked. She hadn't done much shopping for Molly and never thought a few, well more than a few toys and a bed would be over a hundred dollars. Annie pulled out her credit card, grabbed the bags off the counter, shook her head in disbelief, and walked out the door.

"Molly, you sure are expensive," she said out loud! Today was one of the days that Molly went to doggy daycare, so Annie was alone with her own thoughts.

There were days, like today, when Annie could not bring Molly into the office with her. Luckily, she found a doggy daycare, and it happened to be close to the office so she could drop Molly off and, without going too far out of her way, could walk the rest of the way to the office. The daycare was more expensive than most, but the two things that sold Annie on it were the location and Annie knew the woman who operated it. Annie wasn't frugal with the monies Uncle Jack had left her to care for Molly, but she didn't want to be wasteful.

Annie was thankful that Molly enjoyed going to the doggy daycare she chose. As soon as they would get close to the daycare, Molly would pick up her pace and begin wagging her tail. Roberta Kennedy was the doggy daycare owner/operator. Annie met her a few years ago through a mutual friend of hers. Annie never gave much thought to her or her company because Annie didn't have any pets and wasn't planning on adopting anytime soon. Roberta was a friendly-hug everyone kind of woman. She even hugged Annie the first time they met. Annie noticed that she could only tolerate her in small doses as friendly and outgoing as Roberta was. She is the person who continues to talk while you're walking away. *I guess it made perfect sense, maybe she gets lonely; the dogs that she cared for were her only companions during the day.*

The weeks flew by as Annie and Molly settled into a routine. Annie hadn't thought much about the Sanctuary lately. Her new life with Molly was keeping her busy.

Then one night, Annie received a call from Ralph. He was handling the sale of the property. "Annie?" said Ralph, "We have an offer on your property." Before Ralph could finish his words, Annie began running around the apartment like a child. She was happy to be free from it all. "Annie, please let me finish. Your property has sat for a very long time, and right now, the only interest in it that anyone has shown is an investor whose plan is to tear down the house, all of the buildings and let some company come in and drill on it."

Annie yelled into the phone, "Absolutely not!"

"Annie, you need to think about your options. You have had this place on the market for a few months now; unfortunately, the economy is at an all-time low. Annie, this is not a sellers' market. The longer the site sits vacant, the harder it is going to be to sell." Ralph explained.

Sam walked in while Annie was on the phone, and he caught most of the conversation.

"Annie, I want to go see this property, let's plan a trip and go together, just the three of us," said Sam.

"Ralph, please hold them off for now. Sam, Molly, and I will be taking a trip out there soon."

Ralph smiled as he hung up the phone. "I thought she might have a change of heart."

CHAPTER 15

Annie And Sam Prepare for Their Trip to Texas

Annie and Sam were preparing for their trip and tying up some loose ends. They agreed that if they were going to take time off from work, and with the price of airline tickets, it only made sense for them to stay a few weeks. Sam suggested to Annie that the three of them should stay at the Animal Sanctuary. Annie could sense the excitement in Sam's voice. "We could bring sleeping bags," he said, with a grin on his face.

Annie laughed, "Sam, I haven't owned a sleeping bag since I was a teenager!"

"It would be like camping!" Sam shouted in a child-like voice.

Annie understood why Sam was so excited. It was because of his ability to romanticize everything. Once he had a vision of what it was going to be like, his mind was set. There was no stopping him. As much as Annie loved that about him, it had its disadvantages. She didn't have the heart to say no to her best friend, Sam. He very rarely asked for anything, and he was quite enthusiastic about this trip.

Annie knew this was a tall favor to ask. Many things would need to be taken care of if they planned to spend two weeks there. She would need to arrange for someone to mow the fields, clean the house from top to bottom, and ask her mother to borrow some furniture. They would need towels, pots, and pans; the list was endless.

Annie had to admit she did love the idea of Molly having room to run around, even if she would have to be on a lead. The last few months of riding the elevator so Molly could go out back to do her business took its toll. Annie also liked the idea of having a full kitchen, where they could prepare their meals and not eat out every day, rather than staying in a hotel. Sam pointed out that there was already power there, and if Annie would have the internet turned on, he could work on his project while they were in Texas.

It was already Wednesday, Annie and Sam planned to fly out on the following Friday.

Annie decided to take the day off from work; she had a lot to do and didn't waste any time making her phone calls. The first call was to the local cable company, requesting them to turn internet service on at that address. She remembered seeing cable lines, so she knew there had been service there at one time. She explained that it was only temporary, and she wished to have it disconnected on the fifteenth of the following month.

Annie thought for a moment. She couldn't believe how quickly the time had gone by since she returned home with

Molly. Annie's stomach was in knots —thinking about the day she had left Texas. Without even goodbye to Joe, the man she had felt such an attraction to. Annie's mother had mentioned, while they were on the phone the other day that Joe had asked about her. "Your dad had mentioned that Joe wanted to know if you were okay, Annie, and if you planned to return anytime soon?" Annie wasn't sure if she was up to seeing Joe on this visit, but realized that Murphy was a small town and more than likely, word had already gotten out that they would be visiting.

Annie gave a quick call to her mom. She became impatient when she didn't answer after the second ring. Finally, her mother answered the phone. "Hello?" answered Annie's mom.

"Mom!" said Annie. "I remembered when I visited the last time, you mentioned a woman who cleaned houses locally for a fair price, do you know if she is still available?"

Annie's mom chattered on and on about the woman, and by the time she was done, Annie knew the woman's entire life story. Finally, she caught her breath and said, "yes, she still cleans houses. Would you like her number, dear?" Annie jotted the number down and gave the woman a call. She explained to the woman the exact location of the house and what required cleaning. Annie explained that she must get the key from Ralph, her attorney, and that she wanted everything done before their arrival.

By this time, Molly was pacing back and forth. Annie had not let her out to do her business before making the phone calls; which turned out to take much longer than she expected. Annie ran down the hall to grab her slippers and a light jacket. Although the temperatures in the morning warmer than when they were a few months ago. It was the month of May and in

New York it tended to be unpredictable, and it was still early in the morning. Annie danced down the hall fighting with the sleeve of her jacket. She didn't have a chance to get the other arm in the jacket before Molly squatted on the rug. Annie rushed to her, "No, Molly! No, Molly!" she yelled as she ran to the kitchen and grabbed a paper towel.

Molly took one glance at Annie's angry face and bolted under the table. She watched Annie cleaning up the pee that she had so strategically placed on the rug. "Really?" said Annie. "You couldn't have at least peed on the bare floor?" Molly didn't move, and when Annie called to her, she proceeded with caution. Annie wasn't sure why Molly would get so shook up; the little princess had never even had a spanking. Annie slid her feet into her slippers and headed out the apartment door. Annie and Molly were in the elevator with several other tenants before realizing that she was still wearing her pajamas. Even Molly was naked for this potty trip. Annie laughed when she looked down at her. She wasn't used to seeing Molly naked. *She looked funny,* Annie thought to herself. They finally got to the lobby where Annie and Molly slipped out the back door. There was a small section of grass behind the building for tenants living in the apartment building. It was a small area, but the lawn was well-manicured. There were a few picnic tables and even a charcoal grill. Molly wandered around, sniffing every inch of the small area before she finally relieved herself. When she finished, she looked up at Annie to say, well, I feel much better and am ready now. Can we go back upstairs? Annie and Molly went back up to the apartment, where Annie proceeded to make a few more phone calls.

Sam had booked their flights almost immediately after Annie agreed to the trip. But she still needed a ride from the airport once they landed and got a car rental. It was a rural area, and without a vehicle, it would limit them to what they could do.

The vehicle Sam chose would not have been available for delivery until after eleven that morning, which was a half-hour after their flight was due to arrive. He didn't want to wait at the airport any longer than necessary. Sam asked Annie to give Brian a call and see if he would meet them at the airport. He figured by the time their plane landed, and they drove to the car rental place, the vehicle would be ready for pickup.

Annie made the call to her brother Brian. "Brian, this is Annie, your long-lost sister, "she teased. "Sam, Molly, and I are making the trip back home for a few weeks. I have a few favors to ask of you if it's not too much trouble?"

"Well, Brian," Annie went on to say. "We could use a ride from the airport once we arrive in Dallas. If you could take us to the car rental place down the road from the airport, that would be perfect."

"Oh, by the way, I do have one more favor to ask?" said Annie.

"Sure sis, anything you need," Brian said in an excited voice.

"Well, mom and dad have some furniture in the basement of the house. I checked with mom to make sure she didn't mind us using it. There is a Futon couch, a table and some chairs, some end tables, and my old bed. Do you think you could bring this stuff to the Animal Sanctuary before we get there? You won't need to set anything up. If you could leave it all in the living room, that would be great."

Before Brian could respond, Annie continued with her list. "Oh, there is also an old microwave and toaster down there."

Brian teased her, "I heard you were staying there for a bit, but it sounds like you are moving in."

Annie went on, "hold on, Brian, there a few more things. I hope you are taking notes? Mom has offered to lend us sheets, towels, dishes. There is no point in bringing all of that stuff or buying it when we get there since we are only there for two weeks," said Annie.

Brian could sense the excitement in his sisters' voice. She tried to blame the idea of this trip on Sam, but he knew his sister, and after talking with her, he knew better. Brian liked Sam. He had met him at their mom's sixtieth birthday party a few years ago, wondering then why they weren't a couple. He secretly thought that maybe they were a couple but didn't want everyone to know, although he had no idea why that would be?

Annie didn't want to admit it, but she was getting excited about the trip. The warm weather had brought many more tourists to visit New York City, and for some reason, she found herself irritated. She thought it was odd that she would even notice the additional population since New York was already overpopulated, and that used to be one of the things she loved.

It was the first day Annie had taken off from work in a while, so she decided it would be a great day to take Molly for a stroll in the park, down the street. The sun was shining, and she figured they could both use the exercise. Molly had gained a few pounds since living in the city, and her clothes were a little snug. Annie chuckled at her pudginess and said, "Well, Molly, lucky for you, Uncle Jack left instructions on finding more clothes for you when we need them."

A short time after they had returned to the city, Annie

had received a catalog in the mail. Her Uncle Jack must have set it up as a subscription before he passed. Annie knew exactly what the magazine was when it came in the mail, and she couldn't help but laugh. "Dress Your Pup" was the name of it. Annie had flipped through the pages that day. She was just amazed at how many versions of outfits and accessories were available for a pup. She was also shocked by the price. So far, Annie hadn't purchased any new clothes for Miss Molly. But if she kept packing on the pounds, that was going to change.

"We really must start walking more, Molly," said Annie, as they strolled down the street. Annie felt guilty. She knew it was probably her fault that Molly had gained weight. Molly was either stuck at Annie's office all day or in the apartment. Other than the days she went to Annie's friend's daycare. Molly didn't get much exercise. *Did I make the right decision to bring Molly back to New York?" Would she have better off with the old folks? Even if it was the best for me, was it the best choice for Molly?*

Annie's thoughts were interrupted when a young man went jogging past them. Molly barked; she still had not gotten used to so many people being around, especially when they came closer. She was a territorial pup, and her size did not prevent her from telling everyone who she was, and back off!

They did a few laps around the park, basking in the sun and breathing in the fresh spring air. It was one of Annie's favorite seasons; Molly seemed to enjoy it as well. On their way back to the apartment building, Annie recognized an old college friend whizzing past them. Sally was one of the girls Annie had been close to when she attended N.Y. U., but Annie hadn't heard from her since graduation. Just as they were passing each other, the woman turned around.

"Annie?" she said, "I can't believe it's you! I haven't seen you since our college graduation. Oh, my goodness, look at your little pup, is she one of those designer dogs?" she asked, as they went in for a quick, friendly hug.

Sally was very popular when they were in college. She had a slender build but was much taller than Annie, which made Annie a little jealous. Annie admired Sally's long black hair. It always had a shine to it, and there was never a hair out of place. With her beautiful brown eyes and her brilliant white smile, she was strikingly gorgeous. Sally wore designer clothes and carried designer bags. Annie would often tease her, saying that Sally purposely bought her clothes and bags to match her hair and olive skin tone. Sally never did dispute that, so there was probably some truth to it. Sally knew she was good looking, and so did most of the guys attending N.Y. U.

Annie listened to Sally babble on about Sam. The three of them would often hang out at the coffee shop down the street from the college, often just taking a break from schoolwork and catching up on the latest gossip. There was no doubt; Sally turned a lot of heads.

"Have you seen Sam?" Sally asked. "I used to have the biggest crush on him, and he never once paid any attention to me. I often wondered if he even liked women?" Sally laughed. Sally came from a very wealthy family. They lived locally in Long Island, and Sally commuted while they were in college. Annie had been to her parent's house once, and it was nothing short of a mansion. There was a large stone wall that went around the property with an iron gate at the entrance. The gate was closed the one day when Annie and Sam had gone to pick up Sally.

Annie recalled Sam speaking into the intercom and waiting for someone from inside to open it. The grounds were perfectly manicured, with shrubs placed strategically around the yard to give it the perfectly landscaped look. Sam drove down the long driveway, and Annie spotted a man tending to the yard. He gave her a wave as they made their way to the main entrance of the home. Annie was excited; she was looking forward to seeing the inside of the large house. The house was picture perfect, like something from a movie. The house was made of stone with a double door at the entrance. The windows were plentiful, and a balcony attached to each of the second-floor windows. It was a breathtaking view. Annie was disappointed when she and Sam finally arrived at the house; Sally waited outside on the stairs. She didn't waste any time jumping in Sam's car's back seat and giving him directions to the new cafe they were going to check out.

"Sally, this is my girl Molly," said Annie. My Uncle Jack left her to me in his will when he passed a few months ago." Annie had no idea why she was sharing all of this information with Sally. Annie hadn't seen her in years, and she was sure that Sally could have cared a less. Sally continued to rattle on about her career, her recent marriage to one of the most powerful men in her company, and the trip to Europe they were planning. Annie didn't bother to mention any of her life details to Sally. It was clear to her that she really wouldn't have been interested in hearing them anyway.

Sally finally stopped talking and excused herself as she continued up the street at a slow jog. Annie and Molly continued to walk back toward the apartment complex. Annie couldn't help but think of the comment Sally made about Sam. Annie had only seen Sam with a woman a few times, and Annie's mind began to spin. *It would certainly explain many things about her relationship with Sam,* she thought.

Annie reminded herself that she was just as much to blame for their platonic relationship as Sam. Annie felt a little queasy and saddened at the same time, even though she never saw herself walking down the aisle with Sam. She loved him more than anything and despised the thought of sharing him with anyone male or female. She picked up her pace with Molly in tow. Her mind was racing as she tried to make sense of what she just now realized. She reminded herself. *You have no proof, just because Sam wasn't attracted to a beautiful girl from college did not mean that he wasn't attracted to women.*

Annie and Molly got back to the apartment complex, and just as she was stepping onto the elevator, her phone rang. She struggled to retrieve her phone from the bottom of her bag and made a mental note that she needed to swap out her large designer bag for something smaller and more practical. She grabbed the phone and set it to her ear, just before it had gone to voicemail.

"Hey, Sam!" Annie shouted a little more excited than she had planned to sound.

"Annie, I'm going to get out of work earlier than usual today, and I thought we could grab some take out and take Molly to the dog park?" Annie giggled as she covered the phone. "What do you say, Molly, are you up for another walk today?" Molly responded with a wag of her tail.

"Sounds fun, Sam." said Annie, "By the way, Sam, I ran into one of our old college friends today, Sally Dolan, do you remember her?" Sam responded quickly, although Annie was not surprised. Sally was not someone you forget quickly.

"Yeah, sure, Annie, I remember her. She was your friend from college," Sam said in a non-interested kind of voice. Annie thought it was odd that Sam referred to Sally as her friend when the three of them regularly hung out together.

—◆—

CHAPTER 16

Arrival at the Animal Sanctuary

The rest of the week flew by quickly. Annie planned to work from home while she was away, and Sam had made the same arrangements with his boss. He had been working long hours since his promotion and mentioned, on several occasions, how much he was looking forward to the trip.

Sam made all the trip arrangements in advance, and the day for them to leave had finally arrived. He arranged for the car to pick them up at their apartment complex and take them to the airport, and it was now was waiting outside. As Annie and Molly were stepping onto the sidewalk, Sam waved at her to hurry along.

Sam cringed at the number of suitcases Annie had packed. Annie laughed, "Molly's sure does have a lot of clothes," she said jokingly. Molly was going to have to get by on just a few of her essential clothes. A few dresses, pajamas, her raincoat, and matching booties. And of course, her new cowgirl that that Sam had picked up a week ago. Annie wasn't sure where he found it, but Molly looked adorable. Sam joked that if she was going to be in Texas, she had to dress the part. Annie laughed at that. She had no intention of wearing a Western hat, boots, or flannel shirt. But she loved seeing that look on the men.

It was a beautiful morning. The sun was shining, and there was a slight breeze. Annie never cared much for flying, but when she had to, this was the weather she preferred.

They arrived at the airport with only a few minutes to spare. Annie was thankful for that; she didn't want to be pacing the airport with Molly in her arms. She was impressed with Molly's calmness while being in such a vast place with so many people. Sam held onto her while they waited to board the plane. Annie spotted a young woman walking in their direction. "Sir," the young woman said. "My name is Kristina, and I am here for Molly and will be looking after her until the plane takes off." The woman was on the short side. Her hair was pulled back into a ponytail, making it difficult for Annie to guess her age; after careful consideration, she imagined her to be in her early twenties. Her blue eyes were big and round, giving her a look of kindness. Annie was thankful for that. She watched the woman as she reached out to take Molly from Sam's arms. She worried whether the young woman would be competent enough to get her precious Molly from point A to point B.

Annie chuckled to herself, *I never gave any thought to this when Molly and I flew from Texas to New York. I barely spoke to the woman that came to take her from my arms at that time. Molly sure has left her imprint on me. On most days, I love this little girl more than I love myself.*

Annie excused herself from the conversation. She spotted a restroom and moved quickly to get there and get back. The bathroom was empty, so it made it even easier to get in and out. Annie was rushing back to meet up with Sam; she knew they would be boarding soon.

She was surprised to see that the young woman was still standing with Sam, holding Molly. Annie wondered for a moment if something were wrong. She heard the woman giggle and found herself feeling very irritated. *Oh please, this woman is barely twenty, shame on you, Sam.* Although Annie wasn't sure how much of this was Sam's fault, she could see the woman flirting with him as she approached them. When the woman finally walked away with Molly, Annie teased him about the young woman flirting with him, and he teased her back.

"Annie Jones!" Sam said in a high-pitched voice. "Is that a tone of jealousy I hear in your voice?"

Annie shook her head no, not sure of what she was feeling at that time. All she knew is that she didn't like it.

The flight went by quickly. Annie made no further mention of the young woman from the New York airport. She assumed they wouldn't be seeing her again when they landed. Sam and Annie chatted about work, the Animal Sanctuary, and, of course, Molly. Sam loved Molly, and the same was true of the love Molly had for Sam. After only a short time of Molly living with them, she would escape Annie's room to sleep with Sam. Molly would follow Sam around the apartment. Annie now knew where the phrase "Me and My Shadow" came.

When the plane landed, and they grabbed their carry-ons, Sam quickly ushered her off the plane. She wasn't sure if he was excited to get the Sanctuary or excited to reunite with Molly. Nonetheless, he held onto her hand, and he was moving as quickly as he could down the aisle. Molly was already there to greet them at the gate. Annie couldn't help but notice the big smile on Sam's face when he saw Molly. The young woman from the baggage/handler department carried Molly over and placed her in Sam's arms.

"Molly, my girl, did you have a good flight? I hope they took care of you because if they didn't, someone will have to answer me." Sam said as he lifted her to his face to kiss her. Molly returned his kiss with several licks to his cheeks, his head, and even his nose. Annie laughed. *If her phone had been easily accessible, this would have been a perfect photo,* she thought to herself. *Seeing the two of them together made her heart feel full. She was sure Sam would make a wonderful daddy one day.*

Her thoughts were interrupted again when she heard her brother yelling to her from across the gate. Sam grabbed their luggage from the conveyor belt. They rushed through the crowd to meet Brian on the other side. Brian leaned in to give them both a quick hug. Molly looked up at Brian with her puppy dog eyes. "I'll take this little lady," he said, with a big smile on his face. Brian drove them to the car rental shop that was just down the road from the airport. Sam chose a black Escalade with tan leather seats for their two-week rental.

Annie was concerned about Molly being in such an expensive vehicle but, Sam assured her he had spoken with the guy at the company, and it would be fine. The Escalade was parked in front of the building. A salesman came walking out as Brian pulled up to let them out of the truck. He helped Annie load the luggage into the back of the S.U.V. while Sam went in to sign the paperwork.

"Annie, I went to the old Young's farm as you asked. Your furniture is all set up. I must say the place looks great."

said Brian, with a big smile on his face. Annie felt a bit of excitement running through her. She did love the place; it just wasn't a practical move for her at this time in her life. Moments later, Sam came out with the keys in his hand. He was skipping along like a little boy. Annie could see the boyish grin on his face and couldn't help but notice how handsome he was.

Sam's work attire was business casual. He wore dress pants, button-down shirts, sometimes a tie and loafers, which Annie despised. She often joked that he resembled a soap opera star. But not today, today, Sam was dressed casually. He wore a black short-sleeved v- neck fitted tee-shirt tucked into a pair of dark jeans that hugged his body just right. Annie was with Sam the day that he purchased those jeans. She wondered why he hadn't worn them until today. Of course, she wasn't going to ask; that would mean she noticed.

It was a forty-five-minute drive to the Sanctuary. Molly sat on Annie's lap while Sam sang her the puppy song. Annie chuckled; it felt more like they were the parents of a child than a dog. She was enjoying the moment, so she sang along. They arrived at the Sanctuary, and before Annie had a chance to unbuckle her seatbelt, Sam was out of the car and coming around to the other side. He flung open her door, grabbed Molly, and raced toward the house. "This place is amazing!" Sam yelled as he quickened his pace up the path.

It had been months since Annie had seen the place, and it didn't hurt that she paid someone to come and mow the lawn and make it look presentable. She was impressed she had to admit it. Annie hurried up the path to catch up to Sam and Molly. Sam had his nose pressed up against the window, trying to see what the place looked like inside.

"What do you think, Molly, could you call this place home?" Sam whispered in her ear.

Annie rolled her eyes, "Sam, don't make promises you can't keep." Annie unlocked the door for Sam while she escorted Molly to the back of the house, where she had Brian put up a lead. Annie watched Molly as she sniffed her way around the back yard. Brian had been generous with the amount of footage he bought, and Molly had plenty of room to roam.

While she waited for Molly to do her business, Annie's eyes scanned the property. It was a beautiful view. She tried to imagine what it must have looked like years ago before the place had gone vacant. She heard that Mr. Young had passed away years ago, and Mrs. Young was living in a nursing home just a few miles from here. Annie heard a vehicle coming down the road, she grabbed Molly from the lead as they hurried to the front of the house. Annie smiled when she saw Brian getting out of his truck.

"Hey, sis, I just wanted to drop by to make sure you were all set and happy with what I have done with the place?" Before Annie could respond, Sam came bolting down the porch steps with a grin from ear to ear. "This place is fantastic! I knew there was a reason I wanted to come out here! Thank you, Brian, for the furniture, it looks great in there!" he said.

Annie ran over to Brian, standing on her tippy-toes, she planted a kiss on his cheek. "I haven't been upstairs yet, but it looks great from what I have seen. Thank you so much for your help."

"Happy to help, sis" replied Brian.

Brian and Sam continued their conversation while Annie and Molly took a walk inside. Annie was shocked at how much better the place looked after being cleaned, and now that it had some furniture. The wood floors were now clean, polished, and shined, along with the railing that led to the upstairs rooms.

Sam was right about the furniture, the futon in the living room, the few end tables, and a small television in the corner that sat on a stand, made it feel just homey enough. Annie was impressed, Brian, or perhaps her mother had even gone so far as to hang some curtains. The middle curtains were sheer, allowing the sun to shine through, but off to each side, there were brown room darkening curtains, just in case the Texas sun got too hot, which Annie thought was the perfect touch.

Annie walked through the dining room, where she saw a beautiful throw rug. She assumed Brian had grabbed it from her parent's place. She remembered seeing in the middle of the floor in one of their guest rooms the last time she had visited. It was a charming accent. It was full of vibrant colors that brought the room to life. Annie was more than pleased with Brian's choices so far. She spotted the small kitchen table that fits perfectly in the kitchen. Annie noticed the counters now held a Keurig coffee maker, which she was thankful. Annie loved her coffee, and she was grateful that it was a Keurig since that is what she had back in their apartment. Alongside the Keurig sat a microwave and toaster. Brian really did remember everything.

Annie hadn't realized just how much luggage they had until she saw it all piled in front of the door. "Molly and I were just about to take a look around upstairs, so I guess I'll grab a bag to take up with me," said Annie. She didn't get a response; the men were too busy talking about basketball or something like that. Annie was glad that Brian got along with Sam. They hadn't had much time to speak with her mother's sixtieth birthday party four years ago. Besides, Brian was just a kid at that time.

Annie walked up the stairs with Molly following close behind. She let her one hand slide along the railing. It felt so smooth and cool to the touch. She was surprised at how the wood shined. It looked as though it had not only been cleaned, but it looked freshly sanded and stained. She knew that was a crazy thought, but she loved the look.

Annie didn't have to wander from room to room upstairs to find the one that she and Molly would be staying. She knew before she even arrived at the house what room she would choose. Annie could see the sun shining through the window from down the hall. She had loved the room that overlooked the backyard from the very first time she saw it. She could see some of the outbuildings and the pond. She couldn't wait to show Sam the pond. She knew he was going to love it.

Annie set her suitcase down in the bedroom. She was thankful that someone had thought to hang curtains in this room as well. Annie's dad knew how much she loved this room, so maybe it was his suggestion. The walls were light tan in color, allowing it to feel spacious. Annie spotted the walk in the closet on the other side of the room. She wasn't sure how she had missed it the first time she had been there. Annie opened the closet door and was amazed at how much room there was inside. After they ate dinner, she decided she would take full advantage of the large walk-in closet and hang the clothes she brought for herself and Molly.

This room had a double bed. Annie had seen it in her parent's basement the last time she had been home. It was probably hers from high school when her mom allowed her to upgrade to a larger one. The bed was still bare, but that was okay. She had plenty of time to make it later.

Annie and Molly went and checked out the other rooms upstairs. There was a spacious bathroom next to her bedroom. She looked inside and was excited to see the claw foot tub she had forgotten about; it had the perfect layout for some candles and perhaps a glass of wine. The window overlooked the side yard. Annie couldn't wait for the moment when she would be able to enjoy it, but it was something she looked forward to later that evening. She saw a large linen closet and was surprised when she opened it to see that it was already full of plush towels, washcloths, and shects. Yes, she was sure her mom had been here. "Great job, mom," said Annie out loud.

Molly must have thought she was talking to her because she tilted her head. Annie giggled. There were three more bedrooms, all of them very spacious with each having a breath-taking view. She wasn't sure which room Sam would choose, but it looked as though someone made that decision for him. Annie spotted a bed in the room across the hall from the bathroom, next to her room. She knew Sam would be happy with just a place to lay his head. His room was spacious with a beautiful window seat, and it overlooked the side yard that was just as breathtaking as the rest of the views inside the house. Annie spotted an old tree swing hanging from a tree outside his window. She was almost sorry she hadn't chosen this room. She let her mind wander, thinking about the little children that once played on that swing. She knew the Young's were a large family, so there must have been many of them that played there. Annie ran her hand along with the curtains that ran from the ceiling to the floor. They were a deep blue, per-fect for keeping the sun out on those hot days.

Annie was surprised to hear the sound of another vehicle coming down the dirt road, especially since the house sat on a dead-end road with only a handful of homes. She ran to the window that faced the road and peeked out. She gasped when she saw Joe getting out of his truck. Her mind began to race. She wanted to hide. She hated the way she left him the last time without even saying goodbye. She watched him get out of his truck, as his body swayed up the walkway to greet Brian and Sam, who was standing in the yard. It was too late for her to open the window to hear what Sam said, but she saw him motioning to the house. Annie felt sick to her stomach. *What was he doing here? And more importantly, what was she going to say to him?* Annie tried desperately to fix her hair and wipe her face. She had not prepared herself for running into anyone today, let alone Joe. The guy who made her heart race and palms sweat when he was within ten feet of her.

Annie heard a light knock at the door. "I'll be right there!" she yelled. She wondered if he even heard her yell since Molly bolted down the stairs, barking all the way. Joe didn't wait for her to open the door. He was already inside, holding Molly when she finally reached the bottom of the stairs.

"Nice place you have here, Annie. Your dad told me you would be visiting for a few weeks, and I didn't want to miss an opportunity to see you again." Joe said as he studied her natural, non- pampered look. "Texas looks good on you, sweetheart," he said as he leaned in to hug her. She could smell his cologne and compared it to the smell of a fresh spring day. It was a gentle smell that captured her nostrils most erotically. Annie could feel her heart begin to race and felt the heat rising from her tippy toes to her head. Annie looked up just in time to see Sam watching them through the window of the door. She quickly stepped back from Joe and motioned for Sam to come in. "I see you have met Joe," said Sam in an unusual tone.

Annie sensed irritation in Sam's voice, perhaps jealousy, she thought. Joe must have detected it to because the moment Sam walked through the door, Joe prepared his exit. "If you don't mind, I will see if Brian will give me a tour of the yard, and then maybe you can give me the grand inside tour?" Joe said.

Annie nodded, "I will catch up with you in a few minutes, Joe, and I'll be happy to give you a tour. I am so happy you stopped by." Annie watched as Joe walked out the door. Sam stood quietly, facing the door; Annie could feel the tension in the air between them. "Are you okay, Sam?" Annie asked.

"I didn't realize the two of you were so close." Responded Sam abruptly.

Annie didn't know what to say. She realized that she had never mentioned meeting Joe on her last visit, and she wasn't sure why? She was about to go into some lame excuse about why she had never mentioned Joe. Her thoughts halted when she heard a dog bark. It was Molly. Annie whispered under her breath, "thank you, Molly." And with that, the conversation ended as quickly as it had begun. Annie was thankful.

Annie heard Brian and Joe out in the yard, talking. She grabbed Molly and walked out the back door. She sat Molly on the ground and watched her run into the arms of her newfound friend. She sure loved the men, Annie giggled to herself.

"Annie, the place looks great. I hope you decide to stay. By the way, I'll take a raincheck on the inside tour. Your brother here just offered his help with a project of mine, and I never turn down free labor."

Annie smiled. "Of course, Joe, I am so happy you came out here to see the place."

"Okay sis, guess that's my cue, I hope you are happy with the new look?"

"Annie smiled, "Brian, the place looks amazing. Thank you so much for all of your help!"

Brian handed Molly to her as though she were a newborn baby. Annie laughed. She didn't bother to set her back on the ground to walk. She was going back inside to finish the tour with Sam anyway. She knew he was going to love the upstairs. Sam was still in the kitchen, she assumed he was being nosey and wanted to be close enough to hear the conversation taking place in the yard without coming outside, but she didn't mention it. "Hey Sam, are you ready to take the tour upstairs?" she asked.

"I thought you would never ask!" Sam said as he ran through the living room and moved quickly up the stairs toward the bedrooms. Annie and Molly followed. When Sam reached the top of the stairs, she could hear his feet hit the floor as he ran down the hallway clearly peeking into every room. Annie laughed. "Annie! There is a sunken tub in the bathroom. I'll bet you're going to love that!" Sam yelled. he must have forgotten that she had already been here once before.

Annie and Molly strolled down the hall admiring the pictures that hung on both sides of the hallway. There were a few generic pictures of fields, waterfalls, and the ocean. She wasn't sure who had put them there, but it gave the hallway a nice comforting feel. Sam had already left the bathroom and was walking toward the back bedroom: Annie's bedroom.

"I would have claimed this room, but judging by the luggage placed on the floor, it looks like someone already has." Sam smiled as he sat on the unmade bed. "Annie, I am so glad we made this trip. This house is so much more than how you described it to me. I know it needs some work, but look around you, this place feels like home."

Annie shook her head; she knew he was right. It did feel like home, but she already had an apartment and a life in New York that she loved.

CHAPTER 17

A Dip in the Pond

"Sam, there is an amazing pond on the property that I want you to see, I know you will love it!" shouted Annie. Sam called for Molly to come as they followed Annie out the back door. The company Annie hired to clear the fields did a fantastic job; Molly was able to run along freely without the weeds getting in her way and, she was thankful the weeds no longer scratched at her face or snagged at her clothes.

As they moved their way toward the pond, Annie smiled when she saw the look on Sam's face. She watched his eyes light up as he scanned the property ahead of him in slow motion. He caught her staring at him out of the corner of his eye, and he responded, "I have never seen anything like this, I know the buildings are in rough shape, but the view is breathtaking." He ran over and put his arm around Annie, "thank you for bringing me here with you and Molly. I could definitely see the three of us living here forever."

Annie half-chuckled to avoid having to respond. She still wasn't sure she was ready to give up her life in New York. She wasn't sure about her romantic feelings for Joe or Sam, and the last thing she wanted was to move into anything too quickly, or worse, to hurt someone's feelings. Annie didn't want to make any promises that she couldn't keep. She took off at a jog, yelling behind her. "Come on, Sam, you haven't seen the best part yet."

Annie reached the pond only seconds before Sam and Molly. It was already her favorite spot. The sun hit the pond in such a way that it sparkled. And It was so clean you could see the bottom of it. Annic could see the fish moving about so gracefully. *I wonder how the fish survived all of the years with no one here to tend to them, or perhaps someone brought them here recently?*

Sam walked to the dock's edge and tossed Molly into the water. Annie shrieked, "Sam, why in the world, would you do that to her?" She knew right away that she was probably overreacting. She saw Molly paddling around the pond like she had been here all of her life.

Sam stripped off his clothes and jumped in behind her. He was waving for Annie to come in, but she was too busy admiring how Sam paddled around with Molly and how gentle he was with her. Annie watched how gracefully his body moved through the water. She couldn't remember the last time she saw him this relaxed. She felt embarrassed as her eyes moved from his face, down to his shoulders and bare chest. He was so lean but muscular. It was as if each muscle moved independently from the rest of his body. It was impossible to deny that Sam was a great looking guy with a body most men could only achieve by spending hours a day at the gym.

"Annie!" Sam yelled again, "come join us!" Annie gave in and began stripping out of her clothes, leaving her in only her bikini underwear and bra. The sun was hot, and the longer she stood there, the hotter it became. She plunged into the water and felt it splash against her body. When she rose to the top, she was surprised at how close she had landed to Sam and Molly — so close that she could feel the warmth from his skin and his eyes as they danced around her body as though he had never seen her in her bra and panties before.

Annie quickly covered up her chest and paddled to the other side of the pond. The water felt amazing against her skin, the sun basting on her shoulders and face. The water was deep, so she had to keep moving around while keeping her distance from Sam.

Sam pointed Molly in Annie's direction and let go of her. He and Annie watched as Molly paddled vigorously across the pond to reach her mama. They both laughed. *Molly was bringing them closer together; they were becoming a family,* Annie scooped Molly up and sat her on the deck. Molly didn't bother to move, and she waited patiently for Annie to make her exit. Annie could feel Sam's eyes behind her as she lifted herself onto the deck. These feelings were new to her. She was never uncomfortable around Sam; he was her pal, her best friend. Annie hurried to cover herself up and waved to Sam as she and Molly made their way back to the house. She could hear Sam, who was still in the water, yelling to her, "Annie, where are you going? The water is perfect!" She didn't bother to answer and just kept walking as fast as she could while carrying Molly back to the house.

"Oh, Molly, you are soaking wet and shaking; let me towel dry you off and grab you a cookie. I know you must have worked up an appetite with all of that swimming you did." Molly's tail wagged, she was a smart dog, and she knew the word cookie. "You stay down here and be a good girl," Annie said as she handed Molly a treat. "I am going to take a shower, and I'll be right back."

Annie heard Sam close the back door as she was getting out of the shower. She was sure he was unaware, but she could hear the conversation he was having with Molly. "Molly, what do you think of this place? Do you think we could be happy here, just the three of us?" She heard Molly give a little bark, and she laughed. Sam and Molly were bonding.

Annie rushed to her bedroom to put on some dry, fresh clothes. She heard Sam coming up the stairs, so she assumed he had the same idea of taking a shower. Sam knocked on her bedroom door, "Annie, I am going to take a shower, and then I'll whip us up something to eat on the grill."

"Sounds great, Sam!" Annie yelled back without bothering to open the door.

She was sitting on the bed, about to put her shoes on, when she heard a loud bang sound coming from the kitchen. Annie swung open the door to her room. Barefooted, she raced down the stairs. She could feel her heart racing as her mind filled with worry — wondering if Molly was okay.

Annie got to the bottom of the stairs and began yelling for Molly, but she didn't come. "Molly, Molly, come here, girl, I have a cookie for you!" Annie knew it was wrong to lie to her, but she didn't care; desperate times called for drastic measures. By now, Annie was frantic. She flew into the kitchen and yelled as loud as she could, "Molly Hennessey, you get down from there right now!!"

Annie couldn't believe what she was seeing. Molly had used the kitchen chair that now lay on the floor to get on the counter, where she proceeded to eat her entire cookies bag. Annie grabbed Molly off the counter, sat her on the floor, and proceeded to scold her. "Go to your room!" Annie shouted. Molly knew she was in trouble, so she scurried off to the tent-like kennel that Sam had bought for her before leaving the city. It looked more like a screened-in playpen, but they both referred to it as Molly's bedroom. Molly would often wander in there during the day to nap, but this time she was in trouble, so she didn't waste any time going to her room. Annie picked up the chair and threw away the empty bag. Sam announced his big plan for cooking dinner and ushered Annie out of the room.

It was a beautiful night. Annie decided she would sit on the back patio. She admired the back patio almost as much as she did the front porch. It overlooked the fields and several of the outbuildings. Annie guessed that Brian took the initiative to set up a table with an umbrella and some chairs. She spotted a few wooden chaise lounges that sat along one side of the table and a wooden swing along the other side. Annie strolled over to the swing and sat down; she had forgotten how relaxing it was to sit and swing. Her mind drifted back to the day's event, swimming in the pond, her sudden attraction for Sam, and her inability to stop thinking about Joe. *What is happening to me?* Annie snapped out of it when she heard Sam call her name.

"Annie, dinner is done. Would you like to eat at the table on the patio?" Annie loved the idea of sitting on the patio and eating dinner. The temperature was mid-seventies with a gentle, calm breeze.

"That sounds wonderful, Sam," yelled Annie! She went back into the house to give him a hand and spotted Molly peeking through her room's screen.

"Oh, Molly, I hope you have learned your lesson, and yes, of course, you can come to sit with us on the patio," Annie yelled to her from the kitchen. Molly's tail wagged as she ran to catch up with Sam, who was on her way out the door. Sam and Annie sat at the table for what seemed like hours, chatting about the house, jobs, what their plans were going to be for the next two weeks, and yes, of course, Molly.

"I really love it here, Annie, and I love being here with you and Molly," Sam said in a soft voicc.

Annie didn't bother to respond; she just nodded her head. They cleared the table, and Annie was thankful that Sam offered to clean up the kitchen. She called Molly, and the two of them went up the stairs and into her bedroom. Annie couldn't wait to climb into her pajamas, which consisted of a pair of silk shorts and a tank top. She was too tired to bother digging through the luggage for Molly's pajamas. Molly had fewer clothes since swimming in the pond and didn't seem to mind. Annie grabbed Molly, pulling her close to her, and she drifted off.

CHAPTER 18

A Potential Sale of the House

The next morning, Annie woke to a knock on her bedroom door. "Annie?" She heard a voice from the other side of the door. She didn't have a chance to respond, and Molly was already barking at the door. Annie opened the door; it was Sam. "Sam, what's up?" Annie, realizing at that moment she was not wearing a bra, folded her arms across her chest. Although she had no idea why all of a sudden, this was a problem for her, it was the logical thing to do. She had lived with Sam for years and never once gave it a thought about what she was wearing or not wearing. "Annie, your mom, and dad are here. They are waiting downstairs and mentioned something about shopping?" he said with a sarcastic chuckle. Sam knew one of Annie's favorite pastimes in New York was shopping, but he wasn't sure the shopping would be as fun here in Murphy.

"Thanks, Sam, please tell them I'll be down In a few moments, and please take Molly with you, I am sure she will need to go potty. I'll feed her when I come down." Sam nodded and called for Molly to come. She didn't waste any time at all. Annie was sure that Molly liked Sam even more than herself. She just laughed at the thought.

Annie hurried to throw some clothes and ran downstairs. Her mom and dad had already made themselves comfortable and were sitting in the Living room, chatting with Sam. Molly was perched on papa's lap, soaking up all his attention. She did love the men.

Sam excused himself as he went to the kitchen to make himself another cup of coffee. He was thankful Annie's brother had brought the Keurig; although he wasn't much of a coffee drinker, he enjoyed it this morning.

Annie's mom chimed in, "Well, your dad and I thought we would check up on you and see how everything was going? We saw Sam was outside sitting on the porch when we drove up. It looked as though he was enjoying himself. He is such a nice guy Annie; I am not sure why he has been just a roommate all these years? Perhaps this relaxed Texan lifestyle will help bring the two of you a little closer, and I might add that he sure does love Molly!"

Annie was speechless. *Was it the relaxed environment and them seeing each other every day that was bringing them closer? Sam had always worked long hours in New York, and there were days he would be exhausted when he did get home from work, he would go directly to his bedroom. Or was it, Molly, who was bringing them closer together? Molly had become such an essential part of both of their lives now.* Annie couldn't deny she loved to watch Sam and Molly interact together. He was so gentle and playful with her. She wasn't sure what this new feeling was, but she knew it was making her uncomfortable.

Annie spent the rest of the afternoon shopping with her parents. There were many comments made about her and Sam choosing to stay in Texas, and she would change the subject every time it was mentioned. Annie had to admit it to herself; she was enjoying her time at the old house. She enjoyed spending time with Sam and Molly, perhaps because she thought of it as a vacation and not a lifestyle.

When they returned to the house, Sam sat on the porch holding Molly. Molly jumped off his lap and ran down the porch stairs to greet them. Annie picked her up and kissed her on the forehead. "Did you miss me?" Annie looked over at Sam. He hadn't moved from his chair.

"Is everything okay?" Annie asked. Sam didn't respond as quickly as she expected, so she walked over to stand in front of him. "Sam, is everything okay? I wasn't gone that long." she teased.

"Annie, Ralph stopped by while you were out. He said he has a family that wants to come and check out the place. The couple who are looking to purchase the house are only in town for a few days, so you would need to call him right away." Annie's parents overheard the conversation and didn't hesitate to add in their opinions.

"Annie don't let him push you into selling," said Annie's mom. Annie's dad didn't bother to respond. He could tell by the look on his little girl's face; this was weighing heavy on her mind.

"I'm sorry, Sam, maybe our coming here to visit was a bad idea. My intentions from the first day were to sell this property. I love my life in New York, and I don't know if I could see myself living here again. You forget that I spent my childhood here, and as soon as I could, I left this sleepy town. New York has everything we love, restaurants, clubs, shopping, parks. There are things to visit in New York. Look around, Sam, I know it's a beautiful view, but would you really want to wake up every morning of your life looking at trees and fields? Sam, don't you think you would get bored living here? There would be no walking to a corner café to grab a coffee, or walking to the park. The nearest store is six miles into town. And what about your friends or going to visit your parents for the weekend? And what about me, Sam? I would miss my friends and be able to walk to work. What about your job Sam? Would you just give up your job to move here?"

Sam didn't respond. Instead, he lifted himself off the chair and walked into the house with his head hanging. Annie heard the screen door slam behind him. "I am not going after him!" Annie said. Annie's mom walked over, kissed her on the cheek.

"I know this is a big decision. You should go and get some rest and think about it tomorrow." Annie nodded. She was exhausted from shopping and thinking. She just wanted to curl up with Molly and take a nap. It was already five o'clock, but Annie decided an hour of rest wasn't such a bad idea.

"Come on, Molly, she yelled as she walked through the front door and marched up the stairs."

Annie wasn't sure where Sam disappeared to and at this moment, she didn't care. He knew this was not supposed to be forever. He wanted to visit, and that's what they were doing. She opened the door to her bedroom and plopped on the bed. The day had been exhausting, and now learning there could be potential buyers for the place made her head hurt.

She grabbed Molly and pulled her closer. "What do you think, Molly, could you see us living here forever?" Molly wagged her tail, and Annie laughed. She knew that Molly wagged her tail anytime someone spoke to her. Annie set the alarm on her phone for six o'clock. One hour of rest, and then she could have a much-needed conversation with Sam and call Ralph.

Sam was already in the kitchen, preparing dinner when Annie and Molly woke from their nap. He was quiet when Annie walked into the kitchen and sat at the table. "Sam, we need to talk. You knew this was just supposed to be a visit. You have known how badly I wanted a real family to buy this house so they could enjoy it and make memories here." He snapped back immediately. "So, what you're saying is that we are not a real family?" Annie could sense the anger in Sam's voice, and she wasn't sure she should continue the conversation but did anyway.

"Sam, you are being unreasonable. You knew this was just a visit, just a visit, Sam!" Sam made a loud, humph sound and walked out the back door. Annie wasn't sure what to do. They never really had fights, especially of this magnitude. Before she could decide whether or not to follow behind Sam, her phone rang, and it was Ralph. *Lousy timing.*

"Hi Ralph, I heard you stopped by earlier, hoping to see the place. Tomorrow morning will be fine. Yes, I will see you then." Said Annie as she hung up the phone.

Sam must have heard her phone ring, and he was now back inside the kitchen. Judging from the anger on his face, she assumed he heard the whole conversation. "Do what you want, Annie. This is your house!" He snapped at her as he grabbed the keys and walked toward the front door. Annie didn't bother to ask him where he was going. She knew he was mad right now and just needed some time to cool off.

I wish he didn't romanticize everything so much; there are times when you have to think with your head and not your heart.

Annie put the food away in the refrigerator that Sam had left out on the counter before he angrily walked out the door. She didn't care about eating. She had already lost her appetite. Molly, on the other hand, was eagerly waiting for her dinner.

"I know, Molly, you haven't lost your appetite," Annie said. She sat Molly's food dish down on her mat, poured herself a glass of wine and sat at the table. The only sound that could be heard was Molly eating her food. "Well, this is eerie," Annie said out loud as if someone was going to respond. She had never been in this house alone before, and for some reason, it felt different without Sam being here. The big house was quiet, and it felt empty. Annie tried not to let her mind wander as she heard the clanking and rattling of the pipes. She thought it was strange that she never heard any of these noises when Sam was around.

Pull yourself together; old houses make noises. Annie waited for Molly to finish eating, and then they went and sat on the front porch. The sun was still out, but it wasn't nearly as hot as it had been during the day. It was a comfortable temperature to sit outside and sip some wine. Annie wasn't sure when Sam would return, but she knew he had no other place to go. She was sure he would be back at some point, and she was hoping in a much better mood than when he left.

A few hours — the sun was going down, and there was a comfortable breeze. Annie was glad that she had Brian install the outdoor lights. She had forgotten how living in the country could get so dark. The lights shone bright enough for Annie to see across the road. Annie was becoming agitated that Sam hadn't returned yet.

"Come on, Molly, I'll get you one more cookie, and then we can go upstairs for some sleep. We have a busy day ahead of us tomorrow." said Annie. Molly followed obediently; Annie knew it was only because she mentioned the word "cookie." Molly may not be the smartest Puggle, but she knew the word cookie.

Annie and Molly made their way upstairs. Annie stretched out on the unmade bed that she had just left a few hours ago. Annie knew there was not going to be any sleep until Sam came back, and it didn't help that she rehashed the day's events in her mind.

Annie had drifted off at some point and was startled by the vehicle's sound pulling in the driveway. She knew it was Sam, and she felt relieved that he had returned. She listened to the sound of him fumbling around in the kitchen. *He sure is noisy.* Annie heard the sound of his footsteps walking up the stairs softly and then opening his bedroom door. She was not about to get into any conversations tonight; it was best for them both to get some rest and discuss things in the morning.

Annie found herself sleeping much later these days. She assumed that it was because it was so quiet. She never thought the noise of l the city affected her sleep. She looked at the clock, and it was eight o'clock. Molly was still asleep next to her, snoring as usual. Annie slipped out of bed and grabbed her robe. "I hate to wake you, Molly, but we have a busy day ahead of us," Annie said as she jiggled Molly, attempting to wake her. Annie could hear Sam moving around the kitchen. As she walked through the doorway, she whispered, good morning. Sam didn't respond.

"Sam, I want to talk to you about yesterday. You knew when we came out here, it was just a visit. I am not saying that I don't love it as much as you do, because I do. We need more time to think things through, and since we have potential buyers arriving this morning, it doesn't seem like we are going to have that time." If the couple decides they want to buy the house, they will push the house to close as quickly as possible. As Ralph mentioned, they are eager to purchase a home in Murphy. The wife grew up here and has family members in the area.

Sam spoke up, "Annie, we can call this place home. We have everything we need right here. We can both work from home, and we could even reopen this place as an Animal Sanctuary if we wanted."

"Sam!" We are not husband and wife. Living together as roommates in an apartment is one thing, but living here as roommates for the rest of our lives? This doesn't feel right, Sam. I do enjoy all the moments we spend together and the history that we have, but I want a home, I want a family with kids one day."

Then it happened. Sam took Annie's hands and knelt on the ground. "Marry me, Annie!" he said in the most romantic voice she had ever heard.

Annie pushed his hands away and laughed. "Sam, we have never even kissed for heaven's sake, you are getting carried away with the moment, and you need to be logical for once in your life!"

She didn't mean for those words to come out so harshly, and she was sure that in some way she hurt Sam's feelings, but he didn't show it.

"Okay, Annie, if you won't marry me, can we at least weigh the pros and cons of what our lives would be like if we were to move to this town and live in this house together?"

Sam lost Annie's attention as she pointed out into the

field. Sam followed her finger and gasped at what he saw. It was a large black dog limping toward one of the outbuildings. Annie knew she didn't have time to explain and was glad that she didn't have to explain it. Sam saw the dog too. Annie was thankful that the night before, she had left her crocs at the door. She hurriedly slipped them on feet while yelling at Molly to stay inside. Little did Annie know; Molly had no interest in going outside. She was busy devouring her breakfast.

Sam opened the door and ran behind Annie. She thought it was strange that a dog would be wandering around out here. As she ran to catch up with the dog, she couldn't help but wonder where the dog had come from, and did he belong to one of the neighbors? It didn't take Annie long to reach the dog. She approached it slowly and gently. She was horrified when she spotted the wound on its leg. Annie let out a loud gasp! She wasn't sure what had happened to this pup, but she knew it needed immediate attention. Sam saw the look on Annie's face as he approached her. "We need to get the dog back to the house and call Joe!" said Annie. Sam nodded his head in agreement. They lifted the dog and carefully carried it back to the house.

Molly met them at the door, eager to meet the new guest, but even she knew something was wrong as they laid the dog on the rug in the dining room. Molly approached the dog in a loving, non-threatening way. Sam was impressed with Molly's compassion and patted her on the head.

"Molly, you stay here and look after the pup while I go to get some towels to stop the bleeding," Sam yelled as he rushed to the closet, where they kept the linens.

Annie called Joe and got his voicemail. She was so frantic she was hoping he could understand her message.

She made a second call to Ralph. He answered on the second ring, "Hi Ralph; this is Annie; I will have to cancel our appointment for this morning, as a matter of fact, I have decided to take the house off the market."

Sam walked through the doorway in time to hear Annie say, Yes, that's right Ralph, this town needs me here, and I have decided not to sell the house." Sam rushed over to Annie and as tight as he could, wrapped his arms around her, you won't be sorry, Annie, I promise you, we won't be sorry."

***Thank you for reading Annie Jones And the Animal Sanctuary. I hope you enjoyed it; stay tuned for more stories about Annie, her love life, and adventures.